The Roots Grow Into the Earth

A Collection of Short Horror Stories

Bert S. Lechner

Print ISBN: 978-1-960086-03-7

eBook ISBN: 978-1-960086-04-4

TABLE OF CONTENTS

INTRODUCTION

The Roots grow into the Earth. Unseen conduits of **Power**, capitalization and emphasis required, playing upon the knife's edge of tangibility. Walkways for spirits, demons, and Other Things beyond understanding, a weave of uncountable strands tying their dead worlds to our soil.

In this collection, you will witness many strange things: powerful magic bound to people, places, and things; unfathomable entities, some with motives familiar, others whose only recognizable emotion is hunger; victims and survivors, caught within the tangled webs of cruel things that lie just beyond the edges of their comprehension.

The beings, the powers that be in these tales may not be real, but they are inspired by things that are all too real:

The sense of hopelessness lying in bed, exhausted, sleepless, unable to stop your mind from considering all the ways you could seek oblivion.

The sense of overflowing emptiness, the rage and grief and despair that comes with seeing the abuser that hides within a lover for the first time.

The sense of being trapped, caught between so many monsters that self destruction feels like the only way out.

The sense that you are one step from losing control, that the loathsome images your brain torments you with will become a reality caused by your own hands.

The sense of everything being taken from you, your world destroyed, and the blame placed upon your head.

This is a collection that is as much about trauma, grief, abandonment, abuse, as it is about beings with cruel, insatiable hunger lurking between the stars. And, in honesty, I don't know which of those two facets is the more terrifying.

I have a lot of people to thank for helping me get to the point where I can write a foreword in a book. My first thanks go to my family, my parents and brother, for their unlimited support and kindness (and their patience and tenacity while helping to edit these pages). Thank you to so many authors—Rain Sullivan, Shannon Magee, Megan Crist, Maxwell Stegner, and so many others—all these people have been there to help get through the long and often grueling process of getting words onto the paper. Make sure to check out their books and stories if you get the chance.

And last, a big thank you to the giants of the writing world upon whose shoulders I have rested my foundations: to J.R.R. Tolkien, whose books showed me how to build worlds; to Mary Shelly and Bram Stoker, whose books introduced me to monsters and cultivated the atmosphere of my storytelling; and to Stephen King, whose books showed me how to wield words.

Now go forth, and delve into darkness.

The Roots grow into the Earth.

-Bert S. Lechner

THEIR EYES WERE DUST

In the dark we found them.

For years, we had surmised this vague stretch of peat, long abandoned by the nourishing waters of the bog, may hold long dead secrets. Scant clues had survived obliteration of time, scattered amongst the weathered turf houses of our main excavation: faded murals depicting never before seen funerary rites and unfamiliar raiments; stone monoliths, the weathered Ogham upon their chipped surfaces hinting at a network of undiscovered burial grounds and villages. The more we uncovered the more we felt the pull of something below the earth, not far from the original site: A silent, ancient call, crawling through the fog into our ears, bid us to dig, a promise for the find of the century.

How could we not obey?

Obsession gnawed at our hearts. By sunlight and lamp-light, we scoured the bog until we had pinpointed the empty field of desiccated peat indicated by our clues. Abandoning our previous site, we gathered what tools we could.

And we dug.

I cannot say for certain how long we excavated. Months? Years? That span of time is little more than a foggy mire in my memory. Endless days of exhuming decaying roots and dark peat. Countless hours struggling with stops and starts, only leaving our camp for fresh supplies, or for pleading to those whose wealth exceeded their lifespans to provide us the necessary funding. How could we stop? The pull was too strong. The tugging urge to sink our shovels into the mossy, foetid soil until they broke in our grasp, the need to pry the loose clay apart with our hands until our nailbeds bled, was far too strong.

In the end, we found it. An ancient tomb, erased from the logs of history. Grasping at the peat, our fingernails splitting under our frenzy to uncover that ancient structure below, we found it. What a sight to behold, the darkness that spilled from the crumbling ceiling! Absolute and impenetrable, beyond the power of our lanterns to pierce: such a heavy miasma of unrelenting shadow. How fortuitous it was of us to bring ropes despite our lack of expectations.

My heart palpitated with excitement as the shadows wafted into the light, heavy with the scent of dust, forgotten by the light of day. The sound of funerary drums long lost to the ravages of time, the wail of mourners, the pungency of resin and pitch soaked torches, the intoxicating scent of sweet mead and wild berries and roasted flesh assaulted my senses. Drowning in history, I didn't hear Harold's request to hold the rope so he could descend until he was right by my ear.

The rope burned in my hand, my muscles cried out in pain at Harold's weight, but mercy allowed the feeling to be brief. I felt the weight ease with his release and his discovery of the cavern floor. I heard his exclamation of excitement, muffled by the moss and the oppressive fog that hovered over our dig like an intrusive stranger.

"This is incredible, you must see," I heard him shout. How could I not obey? Even without his invitation, I felt the pull of that ancient tomb driving me to descend without any consideration of how I would resurface.

Our Jeep, half stuck in peat and burdened with tools, would suffice to fasten the rope and manage my weight. Forgetting gloves in my zeal to descend, I accepted the burns and splinters of the fiber into the symphony of torment already played by my ruined nails and aching fingers. With surprise I marveled at the gentle light of the interior, brighter light than a foggy day alone could provide, as though the shadows begged for me to see. The design was familiar, a dome-roofed room of cut stone I had seen in many other tombs in our previous excavations. Yet, never before had I seen masonry so pristine, so untouched by time!

Harold almost leapt with excitement at seeing me, taking the role of tour guide within the chamber as though he had spent his whole life there. I swear never before had I seen such abundant mirthful light in another's eyes.

"We were right!" Harold bounded to caress the walls, his fingers bending at unpleasant angles as he applied pressure to the damp stone.

"A whole new chapter begins in the history of this region! To think this site has been hidden away by the peat for so long. It's fantastic, isn't it?"

I could only nod with joy, my eyes taking in the piles of rusted trinkets and mold-coated foods, my ears heavy with the overpowering silence. After its travels, my vision settled upon the figure in their throne, resting in the center of the chamber.

In the dark we found them.

Upon a throne of rotted oak, they rested, placed with care by ancient hands. Amazement electrocuted my core at how well the climate had preserved their body: how the skin at a glance remained supple and young; how the muscles seemed still strong, untouched by the uncaring ravages of time. Their garb was blessed by the same timelessness. With relish, my eyes consumed the auric glory of the gold patterns woven upon a backdrop of regal scarlet. And their face, my God their face! Elegant and gaunt, contentment drawn upon every line of their visage, their eyes closed as if in meditation, their lips pursed and flushed with life. Were we not in a cavern that had been sealed for millennia I would have sworn they still lived.

Shuddering with joy, I gave in to the desire to approach, to prostrate myself before the ancient, regal figure. In my ears, the procession of drums found accompaniment from melancholic, plucked strings and raspy flutes. In the corners of my vision, amber light danced into being from the ancient sconces. Lithe, ethereal figures glided at the boundaries of sight, their lavender robes rippling through the air as though it was water. Half glanced, gilded cups and platters rested in their arms, piled high with rich offerings of succulent meat and exotic fruits lost to extinction. To my flank, I felt the warmth of my companion resting near, and though I did not look, I knew Harold prostrated himself by my side as together we worshiped the ancient seated figure.

I cannot fathom its origins, but in the heat of this joyous moment a dark, cold urge stabbed my mind. In the end, I think this urge was all that saved me, all that has allowed me to abuse your time with the mad scrawlings of my pen. But at the time, the feeling filled me with awful hatred for myself and for the betrayal of the nobility before me.

I had to look upon their eyes.

I don't know why: a rogue, vandal thought demanded it, the kind of thought you cannot believe has entered your head, so sweet and delectable and sickening in its heresy to your own nature. Gripping the trunk of my mind like untamed vines, my imagination cast me into an endless loop of falling into bottomless hazel pools, surrounded by history itself weathering away to reveal the ancient world that I craved to witness. I had to see, to lock gazes.

How could I not obey?

Surprise hit me as I looked down at the noble body resting on their throne, no recollection of standing or stepping forward. Anticipation rippled across the surface of my bones, and my vision filled with the sublime face before me, their regal features eclipsed by my arm reaching to make contact. The skin was warm. I could not tell if at my fingertips I felt my own racing heartbeat or the faint flicker of theirs. With tenderness, I traced their arched cheekbones until my fingers lay pressed against their eyelids. Vertigo hit me, and with the sudden churn of the world around me I realized I had forgotten to breathe. I took a breath of the rich air, scented with woody perfumes and tallow and green herbs. A moment of hesitation passed, and I pressed open their eyelids with my fingers.

Their eyes were dust.

A veil lifted from my vision, one that even now I wish I could have died wearing. Smothered by reality, the sensations of the past vanished, their carcasses blown away as though by an unfelt, unheard gale. In their place remained the tomb, ancient, more dust than substance. Dust. Everywhere dust.

From the body's hollow sockets it cascaded, gray waterfalls vanishing into the dark. Upon every surface it lay in miniscule dunes, a desert of dust mixed with ash and mold. The uncaring, mineral, moldy smell of peat and rotting wood and withered stone invaded my nostrils. Sound itself died, leaving as its heir a hollow void that banged against my eardrums with raucous petulance.

And the figure, oh God the figure, the corpse before me! Revealed in its infinite malice it sat, its skin still supple but bloated and plaid and glistening. Its teeth, rotten down to long, sharp, narrow fangs, gleamed in the wan amber glow of our torches, its lips drawn into the grin of someone about to feast. Though it had no eyes to see, I could feel it devour me with its vision; its curiosity, glee, and hunger pressed against my body with the cold dampness of a heavy fog. Dizzying fear suffocated my mind as movement drew my attention to its arms. Its hands clasped firm to the rotten oak throne. I stared, panic in my throat, at the tumultuous writhing under its skin: not the twitching of muscle but the frantic squirming of a mass of eels about to burst from their net.

A pathetic, fearful voice in my head cried out to flee. How could I not obey? Terror tugged at my strings, a rough puppeteer tossing me across the small tomb towards the rope which dangled from above. The clap of my soles against the dusty stone found a reply in the sucking, squealing tear of damp flesh from behind me.

I felt my heart in my throat as I fumbled with the rope, and nausea filled my stomach as my shivering, bloodied fingers refused my commands to grasp it. The thud of many heavy things striking the firm ground rang in my ears, followed by a scream of surprise.

Fear had wiped Harold's existence from my memory, yet, with that scream, I realized he had not broken from the spell as I had. The sound of bones crushing under the pressure of many jaws and the smell of cooking flesh paralyzed me. Harold's screams and sobs raked against my spine. I turned but could see nothing save for the back of that decrepit throne and hints of movement in the dark.

My hands found their grip without my input. Terror dampened the pain, put a spark in my heel. I ascended, the safety of the mist above me. Morbid curiosity bade me to look down as I climbed, to see if perhaps I could witness my companion's fate. Instead, what I saw will haunt my nightmares. From the dark came a mass of half seen things: giant misshapen worms that undulated across the ground using the stubby teeth in their endless maws. Blood glistened in what light was willing to illuminate them, moans of excitement echoing from within the tangled shadows. With frenzy they approached the rope, sensing where I climbed despite lack of sensory organs, arching in the air with the disturbing elegance of cobras ready to strike.

With a scream of terror on my lips, I mounted the last yard of rope, the brush of their fatty bodies caressing the heels of my boots as my ruined hands grasped the mossy peat. One final tug sent me rolling upon the damp earth away from the chasm Harold and I had excavated, merciful unconsciousness taking me as cries of defeat echoed from below.

When I woke, I found my world consumed by the mauve hue of a dusk oppressed by unrelenting fog. With effort I rolled myself upright, agony etched into every joint. White, hot pain stabbed my chest as a laugh found its way onto my tongue, my eyes falling to rest upon the dust encrusted patch of mossy peat where the crevice should have been.

Interstate

This has to stop.

Melissa couldn't stop beating herself up with those words as she turned onto the interstate. Tall, brooding deciduous trees loomed over the on-ramp, thick branches burdened with dense, dark green leaves. They seemed to strain and grasp at her in her little gray car as they moved in the wind. She could almost hear them screaming at her, *She's going to kill us. Why would you let her do this to us?*

You let it go too long, Melissa yelled to herself through the static of anxiety which strangled her mind. Her foot sunk into the accelerator, the engine emitting a satisfying growl while it got up to speed. The interstate was quiet. She expected people had gotten wind that there was a pileup a few kilometers up: the large LED sign warning '**accident ahead, expect delays**' confirmed her suspicions. *It's not an accident* *though,* she thought. All the momentary distractions in the world wouldn't have been enough to stop her mind from sinking deeper into its hole of dread, remorse, and anger.

Why the fuck did you let it go so long? You knew this would be the outcome. You knew she would ... Her train of thought was interrupted by hazard lights as she turned the corner, uncountable pairs flashing in a chaotic uncoordinated light show across all the lanes ahead of her. Instinct kicked in as she dug her foot into the brake pedal, panicking up to the point where her car slid to a stop less than a meter away from the bumper of a dirty, blue sedan.

Melissa sat in stunned silence for a moment, thankful that the people in the car ahead hadn't seemed to notice. "Shit," she vocalized. *Not a good start. Fuck, how far am I going to have to walk?* Shaking her head to dispel some adrenaline, she put the car in park and turned off the ignition. The gentle, comforting hum of the well-maintained vehicle vanished into a deep, oppressive silence. It was a good fit for the magnitude of the situation she was in.

Hesitating a moment, Melissa looked around to see if anyone was watching: behind her another car was pulling up, sleek and green, the driver and his passengers moving around and gesturing with the chaotic energy of a pack of puppies; ahead, she could see the silhouettes of two figures checking their phones. It didn't really matter who saw what, in reality, but there was still a looming paranoia she had developed when things started to change. Even after Erica found her, after her world became both brighter with her newfound family and more terrifying from what she had learned from them.

Satisfied with her anonymity, she unbuckled her seat belt, struggling to turn and orient herself in the small car so she could reach the shoe box on the back seat. "If I don't have everything this is going to be a pretty short trip," Melissa muttered to herself. The traffic on the interstate was backed up much farther than she and Erica had anticipated, the GPS showing a couple kilometers walk. But even this far out though, she was starting to feel the presence. *Her, no, its presence,* she told herself. In some ways it reminded her of the harbingers of a summer storm in the far distance, that feeling of the air around you becoming heavier and the smell of the first traces of petrichor in the growing wind. *Reminiscent, yes, but there's more to it,* she mused.

She couldn't put her finger on the feeling other than it felt like a **pull**, almost imperceptible: a nagging buzz of static and anxiety in her head, a sense that one by one little strands of sticky gossamer were catching on her skin and beginning to tighten and lead her like some sort of puppet. Melissa had seen where things went after that, and with those images ripping through her mind and trying to overwhelm her, she opened the shoe box. The necklace was on top of the stack, to her immense relief. Without any thought, she grabbed it and put it on, ignoring the way the iron nails and animal bones scratched her skin and pulled at her hair. In an instant, the sense of that pulling force evaporated, replaced by a gentle vibration and soothing chill on the back of her neck.

She took a moment to take a handful of deep breaths before grabbing the rest of the contents of the shoe box. She had made the necklace; carved every rune, set every bone and nail, spoken the words of power to imbue it with its warding properties. Everything else in the box, however, was Erica's handiwork: a heavy but elegant leather bag filled with a menagerie of baubles, bundles of herbs, and more; a hand carved wooden mask, scented with sage, engraved with runes that played tricks on the eyes and almost seemed to move and change as the light played across them; and, more important than anything, a large carving knife, wrapped in rune etched leather and bound with twine.

Melissa had seen most of these things before, watched Erica make them, but the knife was something that Erica had made in secret. Holding it for the first time Melissa was surprised by its heft and warmth. The leather was blackening in places as if it was burning. It wasn't just heat which emanated from the knife, either. Melissa could feel the raw, unyielding anger of whatever thing was sealed in there. Erica had not told her what it was, only that it wanted to go back where she dragged it from and that it would take whatever thing the blade struck with it.

Melissa flinched at the thought, as well as at a prickling sensation which grabbed her attention. She looked at her hands and arms, shocked at the small cuts opening across her bare skin, tiny beads of blood gathering like condensation on a foggy window. With horror she watched her blood drip sideways from her arms onto the blade's makeshift leather wrapping, coalescing into little pools before being drawn through the cracks in the leather.

Fuck, this thing is nasty, she thought, hoping the knife couldn't read her mind. *But what's outside ... it's even worse. It shouldn't be worse, it shouldn't have come to this. The power was in my hand to stop it, but I just let things go hoping for some damn miracle. Fucking hell, why did I let it come to this? How many people has she taken by now? We could have stopped her before she hurt anyone.*

She forced the lurking tears away. Guilt and remorse roosted in the forefront of her mind, digging up memories and tossing them with malicious glee, but with a heavy breath and a shudder, she silenced them long enough to instill herself with resolve.

This has to stop.

Without further thought, Melissa got out of the car and began walking towards the approaching dusk and the sea of hazard lights, an avatar of hatred in her hand. It was time to pay for her mistakes.

In blood, if it came to that.

***

A sense of dread was palpable in the air as Melissa walked along the shoulder of the interstate. With the onset of dusk, her eyes strained to keep up with the encroaching darkness. The sky illuminated her surroundings with the feeble crimson light of an overcast sunset, punctuated by the irregular flashing of amber lights from the endless stream of stopped cars ahead. She could feel sparks of anxiety filling her with uncomfortable energy, her senses overstimulated by the constant barrage of white noise from countless idle engines and the harsh smell of car exhaust.

The dense trees flanking the interstate seemed to close in around her with grasping branches and murmuring leaves: in the ruddy light they looked ashy, misshapen, and lifeless. In a way it felt like the darkness was consuming the very matter of the world around her, leaving only the narrow band of red-tinged asphalt upon which she walked.

There was another feeling, too, intense yet intangible: that feeling of frenzied panic in your chest telling you something is wrong despite being unable to tell what is wrong. It was the same feeling you get running out of a dark basement knowing something is right behind you. Melissa swore she saw things in the periphery of her vision: shadows lengthening against the flashing car lights; long hands reaching for her feet with thin, umbral fingers; transient faces in the foliage of the trees, their visages painted with agony and their screams of pain suppressed by the whispering of the wind. But when she turned to look, there was nothing.

It was clear the other people stuck here were feeling it, too, feeling that wrongness, maybe already feeling the **pull** that would draw them to their doom. Melissa watched them as she sped walked along the shoulder: folks holed up in their grumbling cars, some scrolling on their phones but many just staring, heads all turned in the same direction and faces hidden in shadow; others leaned on their car hoods or against the interstate railing in small clusters, exchanging small talk as they seemed to take turns looking for something they thought they saw or heard. For every person she passed, a ping of fear surged, fear that someone would see the wooden mask in her hand (*or the cuts, or the strange bag, or the fucking knife,* she added).

The pit of Melissa's stomach found new depths of fear and anxiety, however, at the realization that there were fewer people around her the further she walked; the realization that more cars were silent and empty as she progressed. The sound of idle engines waned in favor of the ominous whispering of leaves in a subtle breeze. In the farthest reaches of her view, obfuscated by the gentle curve of the interstate, she could see the trees illuminated with bright, red light. Ahead, too, she could see the silhouettes of people as they meandered like drugged moths to a flame. No effort was required to overtake them. They reminded her of the animals she had seen days before, shambling like puppets towards the already heaping mound of unrecognizable carcasses.

The reminder cast her back into the pit of memory: she winced, recalling the sound of bones cracking as they walked, an alien intelligence driving the helpless creatures forward, unaware of what part of limbs are supposed to bend. She wasn't sure what was worse, the hideous snap of bone or the cries of pain and panic. The sounds and smells of that mound of torn flesh and broken bone refreshed themselves in her mind, enough so to bring her close to vomiting.

But what had burned into her mind the most, what image now reared ugly and gargantuan in her head, was the look of horror in the girl's face at the realization of what she was doing. In her eyes, Melissa could see the confusion and fear. And something else: a sense that something was inhabiting that girl's body. She could see it in the girl's pupils, something sickly black that moved like so many wet towels being wrung of water. Its presence was palpable as it looked back at her, a terrible sense of inhuman intelligence and emotion indecipherable, yet, all too tangible. Melissa remembered watching in hopeless terror, frozen, seeing the girl mouthing one silent heartbreaking sentence over and over.

With tremendous effort she pushed the memories away before those words stuck in her head again. Before the shameful memory of her flight, and of her tears, crawled back into her mind. Her fingers ran over the sharp edges of her necklace for comfort but found only alarm at its growing warmth. It was hard to tell in the dark, but it looked like the edges of the bone were charring. *It's not going to keep me protected forever,* she thought, breaking into a run, trying to ignore the lactic burn in her muscles and the stinging pain from the ever increasing number of cuts across her body.

Melissa reached the head of the traffic jam after what felt like half an hour. Anticipation and relief fought for purchase in her head as she saw the neat row of parked cars on either side of the road: despite the firetruck and pair of ambulances sitting in the center of the interstate, it looked like everyone had more or less decided to park their cars and go look at something. Brilliant red and blue light radiated from the emergency vehicles, almost blinding her, casting the world around her into darkness as her eyes adjusted to the brightness ahead. Melissa expected more noise, some sirens or radios or people shouting, but all she could hear was her raspy breath and the heavy thud of her feet on the asphalt. The silence made it feel like standing in a soundproof room, the lack of noise over time becoming as deafening as a raging storm.

To her dismay, she could see people coming from the opposite direction on the interstate, shuffling in a trance towards a gap in the side guard just ahead. *How many people have already been snared,* she wondered. The people behind her were far enough behind her that she felt confident she could end this before they were too far gone. But these people were too close: they were caught in its web, and soon, it would take over and drag them in. *What happened to those animals is going to happen to those people,* scolded her internal monologue with intense rancor. *How many have already been taken? You could have stopped this.*

Images of sundered bodies, sounds of breaking bones, and screams of pain flooded her mind. She had known this would be something she would encounter at some point, but actually encountering it was different. A seed of panic tried to take root in Melissa's mind, but she shrugged it off. "You prepared for this," she huffed between heavy breaths, trying to be encouraging. "Come on, you've fucking got this!" Tossing the mask aside, she dug her hand into the leather bag: knowing Erica's thoroughness, there would be something in there meant for incapacitating people. Rooting inside the bag, Melissa marveled at its uncanny spaciousness. *My very own Bag of Holding,* she thought with a mild smirk.

Struggling with the bag as it jostled against her leg, she pushed her hand through strata of jewelry, small stones, and little plastic vials warm to the touch. Approaching the cluster of people ahead, she probed for something recognizable, something which could ...

Hey! This'll work, her internal monologue exclaimed as her fingers brushed against a familiar jagged chunk of carved bone nestled among some bundles of herbs. With a burst of satisfaction, she grabbed it, her hand recoiling for a moment from what felt somewhere between static electricity and a wool sweater getting caught on a patch of dry, cracking skin. Melissa wanted to think '*Don't think about where you got it,*' but it was too late: the specter of the smell of wet dirt, decaying wood, and rotten meat invaded her nose for just a moment at the memory. Were there not people ahead who would soon be too far gone to stop she might have taken a moment to admire the carvings as she drew her hand from the pouch.

But there is no time. Melissa broke into a sprint, her desire for accuracy greater than her need to stop moving and breathe. "***Hel gevete noc, se vesra induh,***" she muttered between heaving gulps of air: they were nonsense words, but something about the sounds of their syllables possessed power. The words felt heavy pouring across her tongue, hanging in the air as if given physical form before vanishing in the sea of silence around her.

The bone fragment seemed to crackle in her hand. No light emanated from the carvings upon it, but power seemed to bubble forth from it, her hand seizing and tightening as if the object was electrified.

Only one chance at this, Melissa warned herself. Ignoring the parasite of pessimism, she hurled the bone towards the oncoming group of people, shouting at the top of her burning lungs.

"**Aig guere kthat!**" The words cracked like a clap of thunder; light seemed for a second to be drawn into the bone as it flew true towards the crowd. At the sound of her voice, the people ahead turned their heads toward her. In a way, it reminded her of a pack of deer turning to look towards a potential threat, but the moment was brief as the bone struck the asphalt and shattered. Bright blue energy exploded from the strike zone, dancing upward and outward like branches of a tree of lightning. Melissa skidded in her tracks, unaware her mouth was agape. From where she stood the buzz of electricity was audible: a harsh, high pitched whine like those tesla coils you'd see in a science video on YouTube. To her satisfaction, she saw that the group in the blast zone were entangled in branches of energy, stunned but otherwise unharmed.

"Holy fuck," Melissa managed to sputter, still trying to catch her breath. "You're a fucking wizard, Harry." *Why do you say that literally every time,* winged a voice in her head which sounded like Erica. The joke had stopped being funny for at least a year, but that didn't stop her from making it every time she did something with even a tangential connection to magic. Melissa allowed herself a moment to float in the faint feeling of hope, taking deep breaths to collect herself. *The spell won't last long,* she thought, her eyes flinching each time she tried to look at the delicate arcs of pure, blue light. *There might be more people ahead who you didn't catch, too. Get going: You've got to end this.*

She reached her left arm back behind her, too nervous to look back and see if there were other people there. A sharp whistle passed her lips, and with a light thud the mask was back in her hand. Melissa nodded in satisfaction, and after a few more deep breaths, she continued walking.

She could feel that she was not far off. The intense feeling of dread which had for so long been palpable now felt like a river of visceral discomfort pouring from the forest to the right of the interstate. Despite being within an aura of intense light, everything felt dark: Melissa swore the light itself was afraid, pulling away from the side of the road, refusing to shine on trees which should have been illuminated. In the dark, she could see faces, limbs, and human figures no longer hiding in her peripheral vision. They were familiar silhouettes, yet, at the same time alien, as if something beyond shape was hiding in what it thought was a human image.

Another presence was there, too, emanating from within that pitch black forest. Melissa wanted to liken it to the feeling of static before lightning strikes, or the giddiness you get from being around a crush, or maybe the chaotic buzz of too much coffee, but none of them quite matched the actual feeling. It just felt like **Power**, ephemeral and indecipherable, emphasis and capital 'P' required. She and Erica had known it would seek out a site of power like this: one of the roots that grow into the Earth from somewhere or something. They knew it would try to draw from that **Power** as it drew from the creatures it ensnared, even if they didn't know why.

Despite her ward, Melissa was starting to feel its presence again: a feeling of pressure against her forehead, nauseating and cold, probing for a way into her head with an uncomfortable number of wet, squishy fingers. *It has to end*, she reiterated. After so much effort, she was at the epicenter of the nightmare, and there could be no going back. *The people who are stuck on this interstate depend on you,* she thought.

Her grip tightened around the knife in her hand: the raw hatred pouring from the leather binding, the handle damp with what she assumed was her blood. Taking one more deep breath, pushing away the knowledge of what would be ahead, she donned the mask and walked without hesitation into the sea of waiting shadows.

***

Melissa had assumed the way the light avoided the forest was some sort of hallucination. But stepping past the gnarled trunks of the first trees, the absolute darkness was all too real. There was no gradient of illumination, no slow descent into darkness as the trees blocked light bit by bit. In all regards, walking into that forest felt like submerging herself in water. Blinded by shadow, she rummaged through her bag, searching for a light source while looking back to the road. She was not even ten meters from the interstate, but the road and its flashing lights looked small and distant: a tiny painting framed with rough bark and branches and leaves.

Part of her wanted to go back. Most of her, in fact. She imagined fleeing the forest and sprinting back up the road to her car. Maybe she could go to Alaska or something, get as far away from here as possible and forget about everything. The allure of the thought was undeniable, the pull towards the light all too real, but Melissa knew it was just a fantasy. This was just one being, one place of **Power**: wherever she went she knew there would be others, as bad as this or worse. If she left now, more people would die. Who could say for certain that this thing wouldn't stretch its influence until it reached places where people lived? *And how many deaths would be on your hands then,* she thought.

For the sake of her own sanity, she pushed the thought aside, as she had with many other thoughts that evening. Some day there would be a psychological reckoning, a day where her mental barriers would come crashing down. But that was a 'future Melissa' problem. Out of the bag, she pulled a bundle of dried plants: it was too dark to see them, but she could feel the rough, delicate contours of the strange, fat leaves. Even in the daylight, Melissa wasn't able to tell what the plants were, or where Erica had found them, but in the moment it wasn't important. With one hand, she crushed the bundle and tossed the debris into the air before her. Dozens of pinpoints of soothing, greenish light flashed into existence around her, blinking in the dark like fireflies as she stared with a sense of wonder. She swore she smelled the air become warmer and more humid as they surrounded her in a large dome, swaddling her in light and nostalgia.

In the fresh light, Melissa took in her surroundings. The forest was wild, the thick trees in her vision dressed in ivy and lichen and nestled within an ocean of fat ferns, mossy rocks, and dead leaves. An obvious path stretched perpendicular from the interstate: a trail weaving between the trees; a trail of trampled undergrowth, tussled leaves, and overlapping muddy footprints. From where she stood, it had no discernible end, twisting back and forth as far as the light touched before continuing into the absolute darkness ahead of her.

Though there was no end in sight, she could feel the presence of that *thing* beyond. She swore she could see a pulsing light ahead of her, a beacon of energy which felt both sickening and invigorating, but when she concentrated on that spot in the dark there was nothing. Around her the shadows seemed to push against her dome of light like a crowd trying to push through a door. Her head swam as she tried to process the shapes in the darkness. The shadows felt like they had a physical presence, shifting with all too human movement and grasping with limbs only just out of sight: yet, within the same gaze, they were nothing but the absence of light.

This was the end of her journey, Melissa knew: the weight of all of her anticipation realized in a dread drenched path into darkness. Moving her feet forward felt like trying to walk towards some flailing piece of machinery, every nerve in her legs flinching and recoiling against some unseen, intangible danger. But she pressed on. She found herself in that stage of fear where the eternity of compounding anxiety has evaporated, leaving behind only coldness and resolve. She felt hollow and tired, wanting only for this to be over as fear sought new avenues into her mind.

With each step she winced, the knife starting to cut into the bottoms of her feet. She cringed at the feeling of dampness in her socks from what she knew to be her blood, the wet squelching of mud around her sneakers only adding to the symphony of discomfort. The accumulating sources of pain and anxiety accentuated the tightness of the mask on her face and made her hyper-aware of how it stayed attached despite having no support on the back of her head, as if it clung to her face with hundreds of small claws. Erica had told her the mask was to prevent the being from identifying her, to protect her from retribution in the future, but in the moment all she wanted to do was tear it off.

The first traces of blood on the path proved an ample, if disturbing, distraction from the pain and discomfort. In the green light of the sprites surrounding her it looked gray and unhealthy, curdled ichor in splotches and splatters just big enough to not blend in with the texture of the dead leaves and mud. The smell of iron overpowered the delicate scent of sage from the mask as she stopped to observe the blood, squinting her eyes to pry further into the living shadows. The darkness was absolute, and yet, far off something was visible: her mind told her it was illuminated, but her eyes swore there was nothing but darkness, a lightless scar visible in the sea of total void. Looking at it gave her a sense of vertigo, but she found herself unable to pry away her gaze.

Some need drove her to focus on it: a need to quantify what she was looking at; a need to rationalize and categorize, extract from her observations some explanation. Despite all her preparation and protection, Melissa felt drawn to it, the darkness somehow parting to ease her passage forward yet also remaining the same. The contradiction of stimuli made her want to scream, but the air felt clamped around her mouth like an unwanted firm hand, each change in the breeze caressing the exposed lower part of her face with invisible, prying fingers.

She had to move forward. When the air was still, she could smell charring bone and burning hair from around her neck: soon the bones in her necklace would be gone, and the nails ... well, metal would be metal. Already she was starting to feel the warmth through her shirt, uncomfortable but not yet burning, like a pot that's been on the stove for long enough that you cannot hold it for long. She tried not to think about the pain she'd experience when the nails got hotter. Blood lay in heavier pools on the ground as she followed the path, and with each step, it became more red. To her dismay, the light around her was fading fast, the little sparks dying out one by one. The shadows felt like they groped towards her with some malign intelligence and hunger, tearing away chunks of what light remained to be consumed by some unseen grinning maw. Some instinct told her the light wouldn't be needed going forward, yet that did not stop panic from gaining another foothold in her already embattled mind.

She had to move forward. Walking felt more like backpedaling on a steep and dusty path, trying not to slide down too fast. With one last pathetic flicker, the light faded. The shadows crashed around her thick and heavy as tar, the weight of darkness palpable on her skin. Melissa knew she shouldn't be able to see the trees hanging over her, see the path ahead of her. That feeling of vertigo became inescapable from every angle, the world visible in defiance of reality.

She wanted to look away, look towards anything at all that could ground her, anything that could relieve the ceaseless nausea. But there was no grounding presence to be found. A tear in the void ahead consumed more of her vision with each feeble step, emitting a mockery of illumination. Her sight seemed to collapse around it as if she were looking at the world through a fishbowl lens. Around her the trees felt stretched, their trunks and branches bending towards the force ahead of her: the way they creaked in the occasional wind sounded more like screams of pain, all too human in tone.

The blood on her path, now garnished with chips of bone dressed in ribbons of flesh, appeared to flow forward like cold sap on an incline. Only sound escaped the rift's gravitational pull: the sound of muffled screams of pain and the wet slapping crackle of bones breaking through muscle. She winced as the sounds echoed against the trees. Most sounded distant, coming from ahead despite no sign of people, but some of the muted cries were whispered right from her side, the flutter of cracked, wet, human lips slapping against her ears. Melissa wanted to recoil but could not, finding herself trapped along her current path.

She had to move forward. The tear in the dark demanded it. It was *watching*, looking more and more like a disembodied cat's eye floating in a sea of pitch and trees and flailing leaves, dilating as it focused its attention and curiosity on her. Melissa felt it trying to burrow into her with its hungry, malignant gaze. Pain seared around her neck and on her collarbone as the nails in her necklace continued to heat up.

She started to see detail within the eye's pupil; that there were layers upon layers of colorless shadow lapping outwards like waves of half congealed blood.

In the center stood something tall and narrow, dream-like in its lack of substance. That feeling of raw, indescribable **Power** she had noticed traces of before now cascaded through her body, roots of pure energy seeking some foothold: she hated that she found the feeling pleasant.

There was no discernible barrier to tell her she had walked into the eye. Space, light, darkness: nothing remained but the lies conveyed by her perception. With each step, it had dilated further and dominated more of her view, yet at the same time, it felt ever more distant. Until the point where it was simply *there*. No light shone to give Melissa a sense of color, but she felt a shift from one tone of colorlessness to another. A shock ran through her leg on her next step, an unexpected change in terrain after the eternity spent trudging through mud and leaves. There was a release with the shock, a shiver through her spine. Whatever force that had held her fixated on the eye was dispelled by the tactile change under her feet.

Melissa looked around, head spinning and ears ringing. The forest was dead at a scale that should have been noticeable before this moment. Splintered remnants of old trees jutted at all angles from the barren earth: nothing more than shattered headstones, monuments of life lost. She tapped against the rippling muddy earth, her eyes telling her to expect it to give way, but her foot found naught but gritty rock. "Not rock," Melissa breathed to herself, surprised to hear her own voice. She kneeled to drag her hand across the ground, her fingers catching on uncountable pits and creases and folds. It was bone, though there were no recognizable bone pieces to find: the flesh of the Earth itself had simply ossified, picked at and weathered by whatever called this charnel house home.

A tower stood before her. Melissa could not say if it was the center of all, for none of the world she remembered could be seen. The tower climbed into the darkness, false light pouring like water from the innumerable cracks and crevices in its construction, each filled with impossible shadow despite dispensing illumination. It seemed to shudder and growl in a silent basso profundo which shook through Melissa's body like the sensation of turbulence on a plane. She felt her consciousness draw back from her senses, retreating into the back of her mind and peering from her own eyes with binoculars. When she resumed walking, drawn to the structure, it felt less like walking and more like piloting a car, unable to feel what the vehicle feels but experiencing its movement. Every sense closed around her as her body reached the base of the tower, her eyes comprehending the death that made its brick and mortar.

It was a tower of corpses. Akin to the one she had encountered before yet magnitudes larger. There was no telling of its height or circumference: they seemed to change as the tower breathed, the fractured rib cages and mangled bodies expanding and contracting like so many maws. Ossified insides cascaded down its height like fat, gnarled vines. Melissa could see the broken faces of people and animals: her mind recoiled at their still living eyes as they turned to look at her in the dozens, their mouths doing their best to scream but finding no voice. There was no way to quantify how many bodies were here: she didn't want to quantify it, even if she could.

Melissa felt her consciousness pushing against the feeling of confinement. She could feel the thing in the tower using the collection of eyes to stare at her, looking through her own eyes like they were windows, trying to find where in her mind her soul was hiding. Fresh fear gnawed at her spirit, and she made a conscious effort to shut her eyes, hoping for even a moment of reprieve. *This is it,* she thought, doing her best to comfort herself. *You told yourself you have to end this.* Her eyes closed, she tested her arms and her legs, finding control over herself piece by piece. *You're going to have to climb.* She opened her eyes, burning the last of her determination, and she started to climb.

There was no lack of handholds. Melissa clenched her teeth as she climbed, grasping at ribs, intestines, spines, and gaping mouths to make her way up. It took all her willpower to not think about what would happen if any of those mouths decided to take a bite while her fingers were there.

The eyes in their bony sockets followed her progress. There were too many to avoid locking gazes with, and in those eyes she felt the presence of the thing at the top of the tower and what vestiges remained of the beings to which the eyes belonged. She dared not look up or down: to look up meant quantifying her distance up the tower, and to look down meant seeing how far she had to fall. Her only gauge for progress was the feeling of the tower's presence growing stronger above her.

Exhaustion set in with a suddenness: Melissa realized how much blood she must have lost to the knife. Though she had tried to keep it in her hand, it became a burdensome task to hold it and maintain her grip. After a few close calls, she moved it to her mouth, clasping the leather bound blade between her teeth. It felt like biting into a charred piece of meat not quite hot enough to burn her tongue.

Melissa wasn't sure what to expect at the top of the tower, but her curiosity didn't have to wait long to find out. She found herself at the point where each handhold felt like it would be her last as sweat and blood left her fingers slick and slippery. With a raspy grunt she pushed upward, wrapping her fingers around bone and teeth until one hand settled upon warm, intact flesh. Looking up for the first time in what felt like an hour of climbing she almost let the knife fall out of her slackening mouth in surprise and fear.

The girl sat cross-legged at the pinnacle, still wearing the khaki cargo shorts and yellow t-shirt in which Melissa had dressed her. Melissa traced her small arms with her gaze as they rested in her lap, her eyes fixing for a time upon her broken, dirt caked nails. The girl's head ended just below where her nose should have been, folds of flesh and bone from what should have been the rest pushed aside by an oval of absolute void. It was cold and empty, a space that was both absolute nothingness and a seething mass of writhing shapes. Melissa felt her eyes bleed and burn trying to follow the contours of the shapes in the oval, felt her consciousness dissolving and collapsing into that hole.

It *was* the presence, the intelligence; the presence which had only been visible in the girl's eyes when she had seen it last. Melissa pulled her gaze away, focusing on the girl's mouth as she realigned her feet. The girl was nothing more than an empty pedestal holding the sphere, yet her mouth still tried to move. She was still trying to speak those words which had broken Melissa and driven her to flee, to leave the girl to be dragged away to this spot of power.

She was still saying, "Mom, please help, I'm scared."

With her teeth, Melissa tugged the binding which kept the leather around the knife, letting the metal shine in the lightless sky. Furious, red carvings glowered along its blade, their bloody depths far deeper than the width of the knife itself. Melissa could feel the full strength of its heat and anger radiating like noonday sun. She could feel its raw hunger, blood falling from her face upon its glistening steel until only her tears remained. Her hand was shaky, hesitant almost. Fear gnawed at her: not fear of the thing before her but fear that the hatred held in that knife would infect her, drive her to slay the thing out of anger rather than mercy. Sobbing under struggling breaths Melissa let her gaze take in the sight of the girl one more time, trying to picture her bright brown eyes and braided hair over the bloated orb which now dominated her face. She wanted to say something; she wanted to tell her that things would be ok.

She wanted to tell her daughter she was there.

Melissa tried to speak but found only a hoarse scream. One broken, deafening wail that echoed against nothing and fell silent as the knife sunk into its new home. She let go of the tower, stepping out into the empty air, hoping to find peace in oblivion.

Instead her foot found soft, mossy earth.

Melissa blinked, her eyes struggling to adjust to the darkness as flashing red light filtered through gaps in the trees behind her. Her ears rang with silence which faded like sand falling from an hourglass. As the ringing ceased, a whispering breeze through the leaves took its place sounding like a sigh of relief and a prayer of thanks. In shock, she looked behind her: up on the rise, still framed by the gnarled trees like a tiny painting, was the interstate. And where the tower, where the thing and her daughter, had been before there was nothing but the shadows with their many faces and the whispers of **Power** that slithered like roots.

WHAT LIES IN THE ICY SOIL

What drove him to dig in the icy clearing he did not know.

Into the bank of firm snow, he thrust his shovel, the crunch of uncountable ice crystals against metal pelting his eardrums. Without care, he tossed the snow behind him, eager to witness what lay below gnawing at his joints: or was it the cold? What did it matter? He had to dig. The sky grew only more gray, the sun hiding for fear of what he might uncover. Hibernating, skeletal trees looked on out of morbid curiosity, little more than shadow puppets backlit by the pallid light.

Knee-deep in his excavation he expected soil, but there was only snow. He kept digging. Speckles of crimson strewn within the icy mass rewarded his efforts. In a moment of panic, he checked his face for blood, finding none. Murmurs reverberated under his boots.

Why did you stop digging, the snow whispered, the words crawling up his legs, pricking at his skin with the icy brambles of their needle-sharp consonants.

He kept digging, flinging shovels full of red snow out of the pit, laughing at the way the veins strewn through the ice quivered and flailed as though releasing compressed air. His heart fluttered, exhilaration soothing the ache in his arms as, now neck-deep in the pit, something firm stopped the tip of his shovel. Throwing the tool away, he fell to his knees, sifting through the last layer of snow. Corpulent flesh pulsed in his grasp, webs of veins spewing from the raw muscle to constrict his hands. With a mix of panic and joy he locked eyes with the eyeless mass, its ravenous hunger crawling out of every corner of his consciousness.

The solemn trees, alone, stood witness to his final, cackling screams of terror, themselves shuddering as if tossed by the wind until his final cries died upon the pristine snow of the icy clearing.

The Orchestra

The conductor entered from stage left to thunderous applause. Exuberance precipitated from her every step towards the mahogany podium, her strides evoking the image of a dancer's weightless grace. She bathed in the audience's excitement, absorbed the rabid anticipation that dripped from the gold-filigree pillars and crimson, velvet curtains of the symphony hall.

How long had it taken to get here? How many decades of persistence, of pushing the boundaries of her skills as an artist, of gaining the prestige needed to conduct in a hall as grand as this?

Far too long.

The score's unassuming weight in the conductor's arm sent her mind spiraling back to the night it had found its way to her: back to the hazy warmth of that dream. She remembered Marrowtheadde, its name plucked from some graffiti she had seen on the way home that evening, its long hands guiding hers as she conducted an unseen orchestra in a piece beautiful beyond description.

How real the music had felt and how terrifying: the painful ecstasy of its impossible harmonies, the baleful call of horns, the screams of fear and delight blending into haunting melodies, filling the deepest pits of her consciousness.

A feeling of anxiety flared up in her lungs as the conductor relived her memories. She recalled the panic she had felt as she began to slip from the dream before the music reached its conclusion, the existential fear at the idea of losing those sounds forever.

You could have the score, if you wished. You could play it again, but for real, Marrowtheadde had whispered at the boundary of sleep and wakefulness, its lips pressed to her ear. *Would you like that?* She had woken from that dream with a jolt, her cry of "Yes!" still on her lips.

What joy she had felt upon discovering the score clasped in her hands.

Her mind warm with the glow of nostalgia, the conductor reached the podium. She took a moment to trace the fine-inked title, as she had done so long ago, before placing it upon the stand with utmost reverence. *So much work to*

get here, she thinks, *and now it's finally time.* The soothing chill of Marrowtheadde's unseen fingers settled over her
shoulders as they had so many times in her most difficult
moments. Its eagerness for the performance trickled down
the back of her neck with its every breath, eliciting shivers
along her spine before its presence dissipated to join the
audience.

The conductor turned and took her bow, bathing in the
ceaseless rippling applause and cheers of affirmation, pride
swelling in her chest at the lack of empty seats. Her eyes sailed
over the sea of people, the dim light of the hall reflected in
eager eyes and mirthful smiles and constellations of opulent
jewelry. In a normal concert, she would have taken this opportunity to speak to the crowd, to introduce the works for
the evening. Instead, she gave another bow and a hearty wave
before returning to face her orchestra. She didn't want to
wait any longer.

Silence filled the hall, the last of the applause fluttering
into nothingness. Before her the musicians sat, statuesque,
instruments at the ready. The conductor gave them a knowing nod. In the gleam of the stage lights, her eyes picked at
the glints that belied the large inscribed nails she had used to
keep them sitting upright and bind them to her will. With
one final, deep breath, the conductor opened the score and
raised her baton, the creak of the musicians' stiffened limbs
echoing into the silence to form the opening note of her
masterpiece.

***

So it began.

A murmuration of strings. A drone of reeds: soft, intangible wisps of melody and harmony that defied the ranges of their instruments, sewn together by the dexterous swaying of her baton. A fog of sound rolled past the conductor's legs, her skin prickling at its tender chill. Sweeping her wrists, she fanned the tangible strains of music towards the audience, soft cries of rapture from behind her weaving themselves into the blanket of sound. Chuckles of embarrassment and hisses calling for silence reached the conductor's ears. A smirk danced across the corners of the conductor's lips, satisfaction cradling the back of her skull as her eyes darted across the pages, each note of the audience's calls marked upon the score.

The conductor stabbed her baton upward, a smiting blade piercing the haunted mists of the introduction to call in the second act. With her next downward stroke, a piercing scream rang from the balcony, answered by a static braying of horns. The scream became many, punctuated by a fleshy, crunching squelch among the seats of the ground floor. Cries and retching and jumbled words of panic bubbled from the crowd.

"Stop the performance!" someone cried, their call inscribed verbatim underneath the musical bars reserved for the baritone soloist.

Accelerando, dictated the score. The conductor obliged, a buzz of strings filling the air, sweeping up the growing, fearful chatter of the audience. In the distance, a percussive rapid of footfalls rumbled, panicked cries from those trying to make an exit parroting the flutes as they found the doors barred.

The conductor yelled with excitement as the torrent of melody flooded past her, relishing in the steady climb towards the climactic finale. Summoned with a wave of her arms, a terrified choir of screams erupted alongside the groan of the string, a frenzied call and response of cacophonous wails and nightmares that rode upon the cello's haunted strains. The din of heavy drums pulsed through the hall, accompanied by cries of fear and the rumble of many hands trying to rip open the doors without success.

She conducted on, the flail of her baton carving a white grin into the air to match the glint of her own teeth in the half-light of the concert hall. Raising her left hand, she summoned one final bellow of brass and horns, a sound that burrowed into her chest and burned with furious pleasure. The audience replied, laughter and shrieks of joy and the soft crunch of cartilage pulling from bone echoing in the hall. With a laugh of her own, the conductor closed her eyes, ecstasy bubbling under her skin, electric joy arcing between the hairs on her arms as the music of her dreams embraced her.

***

The music ended much as it had begun, the last moribund strains crawling back to the stage to leave the concert hall a soundscape of dripping fluids, fearful sobs, and silent chewing.

By far, the best performance I've heard yet, whispered Marrowtheadde from the near distance. *Bravo!*

As if prompted by its command, a smattering of applause erupted from behind her, mad howls of satisfaction echoing throughout the hall. The conductor, butterflies of joy and relief in her stomach turning into giggles as they reached her massive grin, turned to face her audience. With all the gravitas she could muster, she gave a deep bow, soaking in the cheers of those concert goers not preoccupied with sucking the marrow from the bloody charnel house of a symphony hall. Laughing at the carnage, she blew kisses to the half eaten bodies in their seats, their hands compelled to clap, their final act before sitting forever silent.

The conductor left the stage to fading applause, a youthful bounce in her step. *No standing ovation, but a thrilling success, nonetheless,* she decided, picking her way through the wrecked human remains to reach the sound booth.

She could only hope the recording of the evening's performance would elicit the same excitement.

THE WALL

In the five odd years they had lived in the same house, Sam had never noticed the wall.

It was one of those surreal recognitions: that first acknowledgment of something you've walked past innumerable times but never given a moment's thought. One of those things that you never cease to notice once you're aware of it. The wall wasn't out of the way in an unused closet or obfuscated by cupboards and a refrigerator. It was just the narrow rectangle of wall along the landing where the stairs turned to continue their descent towards the front door: a flat, beige rectangle a couple meters wide and a handful of meters tall. That sudden recognition caught Sam off guard as he walked down the stairs, still pulling sleep from his eyes. The itch of the stiff fabric from the carpet around his feet complemented the feeling of confusion in his head as he paused on the landing, a sensation ticking in his mind akin to the sound a skipping record makes.

"Huh," Sam huffed in a sharp, sleepy breath. A random revelation wasn't what he was expecting on this Saturday morning. He felt a thought evaporate in his groggy consciousness, a sense that he had noticed something important without being able to identify what. Had something skittered out of view in the corner of his vision? Or had it been a crack that had caught the light just for a moment?

He could feel the information lurking just out of reach, taunting him with his inability to recall it. There had to be *something* that had drawn his attention to the otherwise boring, functional wall before him, but for the life of him there wasn't anything that stood out on closer inspection. He could see small blobs of dried paint here and there, little bumps which stood out amongst the boring paint's mottled texture. A few nails were coming loose, the paint raised in perfect circles but not yet broken. They were things to fix, yes, but something in his head insisted they were not *the* thing that he had noticed. If he just got a little closer to take a look maybe he could ...

The sound of silverware clattering in a drawer shook Sam back to the present. The smell of fresh coffee wafted up the stairs, an intoxicating and energizing smell that pulled him away from his musings. He rubbed his burning eyes, unaware he hadn't blinked in seven minutes. Turning his back to the wall (*what did I see that was so important),* he listened for the telltale shuffle of Nat's slippers on the kitchen tiles. The gentle scuff of the well worn leather soles was only just audible over his own footsteps squeaking down the stairs and the sizzle of eggs on the stove. A smile snuck onto Sam's face while he listened.

Mornings like these were the best part of weekends: getting up while Nat wasn't hurrying to get out the door, having time to enjoy the first cup of coffee. Getting a chance to actually sit with his partner, to pass time together while the two of them waited for the sun to hit that perfect spot in the window and bathe the kitchen in the rose gold light of dawn. *Wish it could be like this every day,* Sam thought, a thought that crossed his mind almost every Saturday.

Reaching the foot of the stairs, he embraced the chill of the hardwood floors, making a u-turn left around the banister into the dim, narrow hallway that connected to the kitchen. His eyes caught the wall one more time before it vanished out of sight, inflaming the nagging sense of a locked away, important memory.

A steaming mug sat on the island in the center of the rectangular kitchen, turned so the phrase "Keep Calm and Drink More Coffee" was visible when Sam walked in. Nat's side was towards him, hunched over the stove in an oversized, off-pink t-shirt and thick, gray sweatpants. Amber light from the stove lamp spilled around her in an aura, blending with the dim, blue light of pre-dawn from the sliding glass doors at the far end of the kitchen. Sam felt his stomach rumble as the smell of frying eggs hit him with unrelenting ferocity. Tempting as the coffee was, he passed it by, sneaking around the island to wrap his arms around Nat and rest his head on her shoulder.

"Hi," she hummed, her voice warm and low, still heavy with sleepiness. Sam said nothing, enjoying the human contact, watching her practiced movements as she blanketed pieces of buttered toast with over easy eggs. The yellows and whites glistened in the light with the kind of glossiness most often reserved to the photos of food bloggers. Sam gave Nat a quick squeeze, pulling away to find his chair at the island and taking a deep sip of coffee. There was a magic to the routine, to the comfort of the dim light and company.

"Have trouble sleeping last night? You've got that furrowed look on your face." Nat asked, kindness radiating from her gentle smile as she brought the plates to the island. The query made Sam aware of the tension he held in his eyebrows. He processed the question with another sip of coffee as she sat across from him, her back to the stove.

"Oh, yeah, slept fine." he replied, punctuating his sentence with the clack of his cup on the granite. "Just had something important on my mind and can't remember it. You know the feeling."

"Yeah, I fucking hate that." Nat said, digging into her breakfast with delighted zeal. "Get it all the time. Can't have been all that important if you forgot it, though."

"Probably, yeah, who knows?" Sam paused, that nagging sense jabbing at him despite the consolation. The need to say more about what he thought he had seen felt overwhelming in the silence. "Hey, you know that wall on the stairs, that's on the landing halfway down?"

"Yeah. Did you see something up with it?" Dim pink light filled the room, a portent of the coming sun. Over the fence guarding their tiny back lawn, wisps of scarlet clouds came into view. Sam chewed on a generous bite of egg and toast, giving himself a moment to put an answer together.

"I'm not sure. I think I saw ... it looked like it had some nails starting to pop out when I passed it this morning. Wondering if I should try to fix it or leave it alone." *That wasn't what I was going to say,* Sam told himself. But what *was* he going to say? It was another clouded thought, hidden behind something in his mind: a mental wall, beige and featureless.

Nat nodded, looking out over the lawn, serenity drawn in the lines of her face as she awaited the sun's arrival. Sam could see her shoulders scrunch up just a little; something she did often when trying to reorganize plans. After a moment she looked back to him, a smirk on her face.

"You do what you gotta do, babe. But if you're gonna smash stuff, can it please wait till Monday? I've got papers I need to grade this weekend."

"Sure, no problem!" Sam chuckled. "I might take another look at it today, and see if it calls for a trip to the hardware store. Got any thoughts about dinner?"

Nat's eyes sparkled at the mention of food, which never ceased to amuse him. Sam knew food was the fastest way to switch gears when they were talking. Having planted the new seed of conversation, the two of them huddled over the island, coffees in hand, eyes locked as bit by bit they were bathed in the warmth of fresh sunlight. The day would begin in earnest at some point, but the two of them made an effort to linger in each other's presence for as long as they could. Sam savored the moment, absorbing the serenity of the peaceful room as he listened to Nat weigh the pros and cons of ordering a pizza larger than the two of them could consume in one sitting (the debate was only a formality, they always got the largest one).

Yet, despite the calm and joy around him, he felt an uncomfortable urgency trying to take over in the back of his mind. A need to remember. A need to figure out why the wall had grabbed his attention. He tried not to close his eyes, even for a moment, focusing all his attention on Nat.

For every time he closed his eyes, he was staring at the wall.

***

Sam leaned against the railing on the landing, his hands stuffed into his jean pockets and his neck stretched forward like an inquisitive bird. Nat called it his 'stumped and annoyed about it' pose, which in itself annoyed him because it was so spot on. *Something caught my eye this morning, now what the fuck is it,* bemoaned his internal monologue, his eyes darting across the smooth surface of the wall, seeking whatever it was that had caught his eye that morning. In any ordinary circumstance, he would have given up by now, moved on to one of the other projects on his ample list he wanted to complete this weekend.

Even as he stood and stared, the green smell of fresh, cut grass hit his nose from the open windows in the bedroom, beckoning him to tend to their own jungle of a lawn. But he couldn't stop thinking about the wall, to a degree where a cold, clenching sense of worry was starting to make itself at home throughout his body. He did not consider himself an obsessive person; Nat was much more of a perfectionist between the two of them. There was just ... *something* about that wall that he had to find.

An itch crept onto the side of his head, another small annoyance to add to the pile. Sam gave it a mindless scratch, all his attention given to resolving the stupid task at hand. The wall refused to reveal its secrets: he knew it was inanimate, yet in a weird way, he could feel the wall emanating a sense of glee at his annoyance. His eyes kept gravitating towards the same spots time after time: the large blob of paint he had spotted earlier up and to the left; the popping nails which appeared to trace one vertical support, also left but more to the center; a handful of dents close to the carpet which he suspected were his and Nat's doing when they moved in. Every time his sight fell upon them, he thought for a second he had found the missing detail, excitement and satisfaction making a brief appearance before recognition kicked in. Looking at the wall started to remind him of one of those 'find 6 differences' puzzles: the kind where the first five are obvious, and the only reason you keep looking for the 6th difference is because the artist tells you there is one.

So where is the fucking 6th difference, he yelled into the roiling caffeine buzz in his head, glaring daggers at the object of his frustration. Sam kept waiting for that "aha" moment, that moment where his eyes would by random chance rest upon whatever it was he was looking for. That moment of true, lasting satisfaction which the wall had, so far, denied him. He thought he saw it a handful of times just out of the corner of his eye, little flecks of something a hair of a shade darker than the paint, but when he snapped his head to look closer there was always nothing.

The itch worsened as he continued to stare. Sam raked his fingers through his thick hair, trying to subdue it with vigorous scratching. The more he scratched, the more it started to feel like it was inside his brain, like some insect had found its way into his skull. An unexpected, inexplicable realization clicked in his head, catching him off guard. Nothing looked different, yet with a feeling of deep discomfort, his subconscious told him a veil had lifted from his eyes: told him that the wall was ready for him to see. Vertigo hit him with the sudden shift in perspective. In his mind, Sam had compared the wall to a blank canvas. *But that's not quite right,* he corrected himself: it was more like a blank, used piece of paper. Paper where only blurry vestiges remained of some erased image, almost decipherable. It just needed someone to redraw the lines. He thought he could see some sort of pattern, its outlines hazy and obfuscated in a way that felt deliberate. Sam moved closer to the wall, not realizing that he did so.

The paint's mottled texture was a dramatic landscape up close, a landscape of bumps and divots and arches and grooves. Subtle vertical lines of thicker paint trickled down here and there, marks left by the edge of a paint roller wielded by a sloppy painter. Sunken remnants of stubborn wall-paper, unwilling to move at the hands of renovators, lay scattered across the wall's surface like great plateaus. *It's just random mistakes,* Sam thought in a half hearted attempt to squash the notion that every detail was purposeful. But his eyes had seen it, and there was no seeing it anyway else: the way the lines intersected with the plateaus, the way the texture flowed, *was* intentional.

A conviction that the wall was trying to show him some-thing on its surface forced itself upon him with an aggressiveness that scared him. A sudden, burning need to touch the wall invaded his mind: a desperate desire to trace the lines with his fingers. Sam obliged the desire, a spark of fear entering his heart at the lightness of his arm when he moved it: in a way, it felt as though something unseen was guiding it, placing his fingers on the wall, using his fingertips to test the texture of the paint in the same way someone tests the water at a lake.

The paint felt wrong. What should have been a smooth, bumpy surface felt sharp with a phantom dampness that made his skin crawl. He felt it give when he pressed into it, as if the wall behind was soft and spongy. His hands twitched at a sudden stinging sensation in his fingertips as he felt the ridges of the paint cut into his flesh. He tried to pull away his hand but found himself unable to, that unseen, guiding force leading his fingers along the lines on the wall, leaving dribbling lines of scarlet in their trail. A squirming feeling of panic at the base of his skull cried for him to recoil. A visceral sensation of terror snared him like a vice, seizing his joints, paralyzing him even as his base instincts continued to scream at him. Overpowering all of those feelings was a voracious curiosity which flooded his mind. The emotion felt alien and cold, as if planted in his mind rather than fueled by his own desire: something about the wall stoked his need to draw and discover, goading him to push onward.

Sam became conscious of another feeling building in his gut, joining the screaming chorus of sensations driving him towards total collapse. It was somewhere between anticipation and nausea: that rush of ecstasy prefacing a discovery that is tarnished by the understanding that you are excited for something awful. A beacon of sickening energy pulsed in his forehead, a beacon he knew pointed to the answer he was told he wanted. At this point, he wasn't sure it was even the original thing that had caught his eye that morning.

Watching his fingers move up the canvas of the wall, filling in details with his own blood which had before been hazy, he swore he could feel that unseen, guiding presence moving just outside of his peripheral vision: a mass of hands, bent and distorted with too many fingers which held his limbs and his eyes with a disconcerting gentleness. The wall stretched beyond his vision, defying the size of the space in front of him. His eyes burned, trying to watch his hand traveling before him while the world around him grew dark. Sam knew the wall had stretched behind him: he could feel the hairs on the back of his neck standing in that way they stand when you know there's something behind you about to touch your skin. Still, he wanted to escape, but he also wanted to stay. The lines between what were his desires and the wall's had disintegrated. It was impossible for him to tell who had control over his body.

You have to see it, it's really something, something in his mind told him. It was his voice, but there was something wrong about how it used the words. His fingers stopped, their tips burning and stinging against the wall. Sam felt his vision lift to a spot on the wall just higher than his head.

At first glance, he saw nothing. Only more of the same dimples and groves of the paint's mottled texture. His eyes squinted, trying to pierce the deepening shadows which coalesced around him. The shape didn't register in his head for a few moments: he thought it was a knot in the wood, before remembering the wall was drywall. It took turning his head to the side for the recognition to hit him, recognition which dropped the pit of his stomach into an ocean of dread.

It was a closed eye about the size of his hand, turned on its side so it tapered upwards and downwards. Was it drawn? It looked like someone had painted it on purpose, but in the same glance, it felt like it was just the way the paint had dried: a coincidental, recognizable feature amidst the rough texture.

Sam tried to look away, to lose sight of the eye. But he knew he didn't want to. This is what he was looking for. This is what had caught his attention when he had descended the stairs that morning. Faced with the eye, the wall under his hands began to feel more like dry skin stretched taut over decaying flesh as time passed. He felt the panicked, terrified desire to retreat into his mind: to find a way to escape, even if it meant oblivion. But something held his consciousness, pushed it towards his own eyes, felt a presence in his head demanding that he watch the wall. *You have to see it, it's really something*. He tried to rationalize what he was experiencing, tried to convince himself he must be dreaming despite knowing that he was awake.

A scream died in Sam's mouth as the eye opened, the paint peeling to the sides like bloated eyelids with a sickening smack akin to the sound of wet lips. In the whites of the eye, he could see the torn edges of floral wallpaper and the smooth surface of the bone-white drywall. Pulsing red veins grew and shrank and slithered in place across the whites of the eye, but it was the pupil that grabbed his attention most. The shape was unrecognizable. He felt his eyes lose focus as he tried to pin down its ever changing dimensions. Moisture dripped down his cheeks, filling his nose with the sharp scent of rust.

The eye stared at him, unblinking, burning into him with an unfathomable sense of coldness. Long fingers with too many joints and too many teeth squirmed from the void within the pupil, grasping for his face. *It isn't a void,* a voice told him, borrowing his own voice and drawing words from his memory like you would pull scraps of paper from a hat. Looking again, he saw emaciated figures staring back at him from within the pupil, their features cast in shadow, their bodies backlit by an ash choked fog that burned red and angry in some eternal dusk. Though he could not see their eyes, he could feel their gaze carving into him with uncompromising hunger. His skin tried to back away from the cold, gritty touch of those long fingers on his cheeks, their teeth digging into his flesh.

Sam, said the wall: the voice was familiar, a gentle, soothing voice which vibrated through his bones.

Sam, "Hey, Sam! Where are you?"

Sam blinked. It was the first time he could remember blinking since he started looking at the wall. His legs buckled, sending him backward into the stair railing, almost winding him. In an instant, he felt an oppressive fog evaporate from his consciousness, the world fading out of focus in a dizzying haze. For a moment, he saw the extent of the crimson lines he had drawn, surrounding the eye in a lattice of blood. Understanding struck for a second before it was washed away by Nat's repeated, distant call.

"Hey, Sam! Where are you?"

Sam forced himself to blink a few more times, his eyes taking on a sandpaper consistency against the backs of his eyelids. The wall stood before him in all its beige blandness. He tested his fingers against each other, unable to find even a scratch while open wires of confusion in his head tried to connect and form a cohesive thought.

"I'm ... ugh, fuck," Sam tried to say, his voice unable to resonate through the dryness in his throat. He swallowed, moving his tongue around his mouth to seek additional moisture. "I was just in the bathroom, coming downstairs now. What's up?" The lie slipped through his teeth with no effort.

"You ok if we go with some olives on the pizza tonight? It's, like, an extra dollar or something." The normality of Nat's query sounded artificial, almost like a thin, plastic sheet shrouding reality. Sam shook his head, breathing deep breaths while aftershocks of fear rocked his core. Was that a hallucination? A vision? Sam checked his phone: 17:07. *I stood here for 8 hours,* echoed a voice in his head, a voice he couldn't be sure was his. Dumbfounded shock filled his body, fighting for space with the confusion and fear in his mind. The sound of his heart beating raged his ears, its relentless staccato almost deafening him.

"That's fine, hun. I'll order in 20 or so." Sam managed to reply, thinking he must have sounded shaky. He hated the feeling of the roadblock in his head stopping him from running to her, trying to convey what he had seen. *She won't understand,* his internal monologue told him, *she hasn't seen. Maybe you should make her see.*

The thought felt like it came out of nowhere, the malice in that last sentence making his skin crawl. His mind could picture setting Nat in his place to stare at the wall, to see what he saw: to let her be pulled into the eye by those rending fingers and join the figures in that ashy space beyond. That he could conjure that sort of thought, that the thought made him feel good, made him recoil in horror at himself. He tried to force the thought out, shaking his head again, taking the first ginger steps towards the stair down from the landing. Reaching the edge of the first step, he turned to look at the wall again, to confirm its normalcy. Upon the blank canvas of that wall, impossible to miss, was the shape of the closed eye drawn in the texture of the paint. Closed, but still watching.

With a spark of fear at his heels, Sam sprinted down the stairs with a renewed energy, seeking the light and comfort of the kitchen, fixing his vision on his feet lest the eye open once more.

***

Sam found little rest Saturday night.

In the dark, time took on an overwhelming heaviness, crushing his chest as his mind projected the day's memories upon the ceiling. Distorted images of the wall filled his vision in a relentless loop: its beige surface darkened by emaciated silhouettes, its single eye consuming his spirit with its gaze, reaching forth with those horrible, toothy fingers. He wanted to think about anything else. About the perfectness of the dawn that morning, about the mirthful bubble of Nat's laugh and the soft comfort of her body as they cuddled on the couch and watched ...

What did we watch? Sam asked himself, the question vanishing into the rolling seas of anxiety in his mind. Panic sparked in him at the inability to recall what had been on that tiny screen not an hour ago: all he could imagine was a blank, beige screen with textures all too familiar. A soft whisper crept into his thoughts. In the thick silence of the night, the voice almost sounded like it came from a mouth pressed against his ear, its cracked lips sputtering warm droplets of ichor with every word.

We were watching the wall. Didn't you see it?

"It was quite something," he found himself replying out loud, goosebumps rising on his skin at the genuineness of the thought. It felt wrong, out of place, incongruous with the terror he knew he remembered, and yet, it *was* his own thought. *No. No part of what you saw was right, why did you say that?* Sam tried to retort in his head, a flailing sense of desperation condensing at the base of his skull as he struggled against this newest intrusive thought. He could feel the wall watching him with a palpable, malicious glee as it reveled in his internal struggle: the way it looked at him felt not unlike the way a spider watches its prey, entangled and envenomed, waiting until their meal is done squirming to move in and feast. The Wall's alien consciousness pushed against his body with an unbearable, cold, gritty wetness that sunk into his skin and pried its way behind his eyes.

From where he lay, Sam was able to see out the open door into the thick darkness of the stairwell beyond. Looking past that doorway the nothingness felt like an oceanic abyss: a threatening world of impenetrable void concealing unseen, hungry things just out of sight. Even through the shadows, he could see the lines drawn in blood across the wall's surface, darker than the darkness, crawling in place with an almost imperceptible ticking of uncountable fingernails. The lines beseeched him with plaintive whispers to trace his fingers across them once again, to finish the lattice and accept the wall's chilling touch. Their guttural words filled his ears like mud: thick, harsh, unfamiliar sounds that were meaningless yet filled with a sensation of power he could neither describe nor understand.

Fear bubbled up in his chest as he found himself muttering those words, feeling the taste of rust coat his tongue as they crawled from his throat. The words seemed to hang in the air, prickling his skin and making his hair stand straight as if a lightning strike were nigh. A burning desire filled him to leave the bed and obey the wall and the whispering lines: to feel again that caress of those toothy fingers, to let them draw him into the world of ash.

A terrible curiosity snuck into his mind as he wondered whether his blood alone would be enough to finish the lines. *Nat is fast asleep,* whispered a mockery of his voice in his head, quiet among the raging thoughts and yet overpowering. From the darkness, Sam could see the white eye gleaming, peeking up from below the railing with palpable excitement. He could feel the wall leading him on, driving him to pursue that line of thought. *She's a heavy sleeper, it would take no effort to just ...*

In vivid detail, Sam imagined sneaking from the bed to the kitchen. Watched himself pick out a knife. Rehearsed finding and cleaning the bucket in the broom closet they had bought when the sink was leaking a year back. *It would take no effort,* the voice in his head repeated with sickening malevolence.

It really wouldn't, would it, he replied, horrified at how right the thought felt. The compulsion to see the dark thoughts through, to allow them to have a platform in his head, squeezed his mind like a clamp. Helplessness filled him at the return of the lightness of his body, the feeling of something out of his control guiding him to act out thoughts that were not his. His mind told him (*no, the wall told him*) that if he followed through this torment would end. Sam looked over to Nat, her back facing him, the side of her chest rising in gentle waves with each breath. He felt the desperate desire to hold her, to clasp her tight and sink his face into her hair as he had done so many times to stave off the terrors of the night. Yet fear held him to the bed like tar: a fear of what his hands would do if he put them anywhere near her.

You don't want to hurt Nat, Sam yelled into his tortured mind, hoping contradicting the awful desire would push it away. *It's not your desire,* "You don't want to hurt her." The thoughts turned to whispers by instinct, hopeless pleas cast into the night: desperate wishes that something good was listening. "You don't want to hurt her, you don't. "

With a concerted effort, Sam turned his back to Nat and wrapped his arms around his chest, gripping himself with a firmness fueled by unrelenting panic while the silent night echoed with his thunderous heartbeat. Repeating his mantra, he rocked himself back and forth, weeping between whispers until exhaustion took him while the eye of the wall looked on with an unsettling air of satisfaction, unblinking and merciless.

***

When sleep did take him into its heavy embrace, Sam found himself haunted by a solitary, vivid dream.

Stood upon a precipice his gaze fell across endless vistas of ashen snow, their furthest distances obscured by all consuming, hazy-red clouds of some perpetual storm. Weathered ruins grew along the smooth, ruddy-gray hills like crooked rows of serrated, broken teeth: ancient skyscrapers whose decomposing steel skeletons felt alien, and yet, all too familiar. With the nonchalance of dream logic, Sam's mind told him this was the world he had seen in the depths of that ever shifting pupil. With the knowledge came a strange feeling of dry, sinking calmness that blanketed his mind in a soothing balm as he stared upon the wasteland: a sense of belonging and safety which felt incongruous with the desolation before him. "This is my home," he felt himself say, his mouth struggling to move in the heaviness of the dreamy air, the words echoing in his ears.

A sensation of movement in the corner of his vision led him to look down, leaning over a rusted, steel railing which had not been there before. Surrounding his lookout point, seas of bony shadows swayed in the soft currents of an unfelt wind like strange kelp, their almost human forms gazing up in unison like fields of rotting, disfigured sunflowers. In the dusklight, their eyes gleamed with a sickening brilliance, uncountable disks of silver set in disconcerting clusters upon their faces. Looking down upon the shadowy throng brought upon Sam a profound feeling of sadness he could not quite explain.

Curiosity drove Sam to follow their gaze, a terrible shock-wave of awe filling his mind as his own eyes were drawn upwards towards the sky. In a fraction of a moment, he realized it was not a haze of dusky clouds that filled the horizon and air above: it was a dead sun, corpulent and red, shedding scraps of sickly plasma the way a burn victim sheds their melted skin and charred flesh. No heat or light radiated from that solar cadaver, but rather a jarring mockery of cold illumination which lit the world in shadow. As he gazed upon the sun, Sam could hear it screaming, crying out in agony even after death:

a crunching, static wail that grated against his skull like two coarse rocks being ground together. He tried to press his hands against his ears but found no respite, the death cry filling the space around him like thick grains of sand filling an hourglass. From below, a reply to the dead sun's scream rose from the sea of shadows, a raspy hiss like a field of grass in the winds that portent a storm.

The dream winds picked up, gentle and cold upon Sam's face but fouled by the dry, earthy sweet smell of thick mold. There was another scent upon the wind, too, a scent that clung to the back of his throat which seemed to twist and change each time he came close to finding some vague sense of recognition. Before he could process the sensation, the wind accelerated as if pursued by a predator, whistling and howling through the shattered grins of the ruined build-ings as darkness spread in the horizon. The hissing of the crowd below crescendoed into a chattering, gnashing moan of terror to match the solar screams and the horrible wind. The darkness took shape, and Sam, too, let out a piercing scream when the recognition hit him.

His small, helpless voice joined the terrible dirge of this dead world and its rotting sun as the cadaverous star was eclipsed by a colossal hand: a human hand darker than the void, its fingers too long and too numerous, squirming with shapeless hungry things and shifting inhuman faces ...

Sam woke to the light of early dawn, the scream still on his lips. In a flash, he turned to Nat seeking comfort despite his thoughts in the wakeful hours of the night. But he was not in his bed.

He was curled up on the landing with his face to the wall.

***

For a solid five minutes, Sam thought he was having a heart attack: whether it was an aftershock of the dream or waking up in front of the wall, he couldn't tell. Heavy pulses shook his body with every heartbeat, the throbbing feeling in his veins punctuating his shallow breaths. Paralysis kept him trapped in the fetal position, staring at the wall, jagged faces etched with mockery staring back before fading into the texture of the paint. His skin tightened as chilling imagery and terrible questions cracked through the thick mud of panic in his head. *What did I do in my sleep? Oh God, Nat ...*

There was no blood on the wall, no sign of crimson on the white carpet, but something told Sam the wall wouldn't allow any traces to remain. Fighting against his shaking body, he unclasped his right hand from around his leg, wincing at the stiffness and tension held in his joints as he brought his palm into view. *No signs of blood here either,* Sam told himself, trying to find passage out of his panic.

Without success, he tried to still his body and regain control of his breathing, his mind still stuck imagining what he might find should he go back upstairs to the bedroom: he could visualize climbing the stairs to see a raised lump in the blankets with crystal clarity as if it was a traumatic memory. Peeling away the covers, he saw Nat, lying exsanguinated beneath with fear and confusion written upon her lifeless face.

The sound of the fridge door banging shut below shocked Sam out of his imagination. He froze, listening as the delicate shuffle of Nat's slippers became only just audible from the kitchen. Despite the ferocity of the shaking through his body, he pushed himself up onto his knees, taking deep breaths as he listened for more reassuring sounds from below. Part of him was willing to believe what he heard, was willing to shake off the nightmares and the dark thoughts and go downstairs. To try and pretend it was just another Sunday. Most of his mind, however, was poisoned with doubt. Looking at the wall, staring at the eye in the paint which glared at him even when closed, he could not escape the feeling that it was still toying with him: planting fresh hopes only to crush them again. To tighten its hold over him until nothing remained but the need to draw the lines.

Nausea clawed at him when Sam tried to stand, accompanied by the kind of dizziness you get after drinking too much. The railing became his perch for a moment, his stom-

ach and his brain debating over the pros and cons of vomiting. From where he stood, he could see their bed in its
morning disarray: among the chaotic waves of blankets there
was no sign of Nat. A meager drop of relief sunk in, just
enough to let Sam take a deep breath and reclaim some
semblance of control over his body. With a few deep breaths
more he pushed aside the dizziness. Finding the confidence
to descend the stairs, he made his way down the hall, a greater
splash of relief hitting him as the wall disappeared from view.

There was a disconcerting mundane quality to the
kitchen: a sensation that the 'normal' he could see was nothing more than flimsy wallpaper hiding some terrible truth.
Or is it more like the set of a tv show, asked Sam's internal
monologue. A headache trickled across his temple when he
tried to make sense of the feeling. Anxiety prickled the back
of his head at the thought that, in a way, the broken, ashy
world in his dream was more real than the kitchen before
him.

Nat sat in her favorite spot on the left of the island,
hunched over her cup of coffee and plate of cold pizza. The
sharp illumination of her phone highlighted the smile lines
on her face: in the waxing light of dawn, she looked almost
statuesque, a modern Thinking Man absorbed in deep contemplation of memes. *How did she not notice me on the landing,* he asked himself, watching her with suspicion. *Maybe
the wall has gotten to her as well.* Seeing her, summoned a

throng of fears into his mind as he made cautious steps across the tile floor: fear that she was nothing but an illusion, that touching her would cast him out of one last blissful dream. Fear that the intrusive thoughts cultivated by the wall would spring back into the forefront and take over his actions. Even by fearing them, he could feel the sickening images forming in rank and file in the back of his head, waiting for some mental Trojan Horse to let them in.

She noticed him before he made it halfway across the kitchen, the familiar sparkle of cheeky mirth kindling in her eyes as her mouth stretched into a grin.

"Hey there, sleepyhead! You almost missed the sunrise."

An unexpected surge of anger kindled in his stomach for one brief moment at her playful jab. After all the horrors and the dark dreams, the response felt dismissive and condescending. His eyes gravitated towards the drawer where they kept the knives before he caught himself, the sudden rage turning to guilt in an instant. For a brief moment amidst the jarring shift of emotions, Sam swore he felt something wet, something with too many fingers, retreating from the top of his brain and back into his subconscious. *It almost had you, you almost did it,* said a voice in his head: he couldn't tell whether the voice was chastising or mocking him.

A need to go to Nat struck him despite everything he feared: a need to prove she was real and to seek her comfort. It was enough to push Sam past his hesitation and his dark thoughts. He rushed to Nat and wrapped his arms around her shoulder in a heavy embrace, a tidal wave of relief drowning his anxiety for a blissful second as he felt Nat's body soften and lean into the deep hug. He pressed his head into the crook between her neck and shoulder, feeling the softness of her hair on his face, letting it stick to his tear-dampened cheek. For the first time in what felt like an eternity, there was a sense of safety, even as the flood of relief abated and the first sharp tips of anxiety began to resurface.

"Aww, you're so sweet," Nat hummed in her soothing morning voice. With a tender wiggle she unfurled her arms and wrapped herself around Sam. "Is everything ok?"

"Mhm," Sam replied, buying himself more time to answer the question. *Where do I even begin,* he thought to himself. *How do you tell someone that you were imagining hurting them?* Despite an overpowering feeling of reluctance, he let go of Nat with a parting kiss on her cheek. His favorite mug rested on the island, the coffee Nat had poured no longer steaming: a lingering sensation of regret prevented him from checking the time. Finding his seat, he hoisted the mug to his lips, ignoring that the text had changed to say "Keep Calm and Watch the Wall."

After a thoughtful sip, Sam found a proper reply to Nat's question, filtered and curated to avoid the truth. "Yeah, I was tossing and turning real bad last night. Lots going on in my mind, I guess." *Understatement of the year,* he thought.

Nat responded with a knowing nod, reaching across the table for his hand. "I'm sorry, babe, that really sucks. Is Keith being an asshole and sending those weekend emails again?"

It was an out: the perfect lead for a white lie. "Yeah," replied Sam as he distracted himself by grabbing a slice of pizza from the fridge, "he's been insufferable about the project we're starting next week. Going on about how much our jobs are on the line and all that stupid bullshit. Guess it's getting to me more than I expected."

Again Nat responded with a nod. "Jeez. Fuck Keith, seriously. Have you changed your mind about letting me give him a piece of my mind yet?"

"Hah, I might just take you up on that someday." said Sam with a forced chuckle. He loved the feisty vitriol in her tone of voice whenever she went on the warpath. She never quite got to the point of full-on anger, but once more Sam found himself glad he wasn't one of her more difficult students (or Keith, for that matter).

The moment of conversation passed: even with the guilt of deception and the pain of holding back his feelings, that small moment of talking had felt like a portal back to normality. He took another sip of coffee. "Keep Calm and Watch the Wall" said the mug. In the reflection upon its glossy surface, the fridge was gone: in its place was the wall, the gaze of its all too familiar eye glaring at him with an air of sadistic joy. Sam sighed, part from exhaustion and part from dismay. *Guess you were going to show up eventually this morning,* he thought. In his peripheral vision, he could see that Nat had returned to looking at her phone. He could feel the wall taunting him to contemplate the knives and their resting place.

With a disturbing lightness, the awful images clawed their way back into his head, lurking in the shadows of his conscious thoughts. *It's not going to go away,* whispered voices in his head with an air of weary remorse. Some were his, others were Nat, his parents, even Keith: the wall knew them all and wore them like masks to hide its true voice. *You're going to keep seeing it, keep feeling it. Eventually, you'll be too tired to stop it. The wall's going to catch you off guard, and you're going to go for those knives. Deep down you know you really want to do it. Don't you?* He blinked a few times, hoping the text on the mug would stop saying "Keep Calm and Grab a Knife." Visions of the weeks ahead fluttered within his mind: an endless parade of sleepless, tormented nights and dreams of dead worlds; long days filled with exhaustion, anxiety, and fear. *It's only a matter of time.*

He knew the voices were right. He wouldn't be able to look at a knife again without thinking of what awful acts he could do with it. Even with the ever growing light of the dawn, the kitchen felt dark, as if the air was filled with shadowy mist. A sense of hopeless amusement overcame him at how far he had fallen in only a day: *this must be what going insane feels like,* joked his inner monologue. In the reflection of his mug, he made eye contact with the wall, staring head on into that ever shifting, enigmatic pupil. In its fluctuating depths, he saw the ways the day could end as if in an act of mercy the wall was giving him a choice.

To Sam, with his dark thoughts becoming burning desires, the decision was a no brainer.

A little memory snuck into his head watching Nat out of the corner of his eye: *she was sitting like that when we met.* The fuzzy, warm feeling of reminiscence wafted through his consciousness remembering seeing her for the first time. It was the feeling he always imagined getting on his deathbed: one final parade of happy memories before oblivion. *It was a book, not a phone, but she was sitting just like that.*

Yeah, Sam replied to himself, *It was the only table without a lot of people.* The sound of her first "Hey," wandered into his head: the hovering kindness in that single word, the way her eyes had welcomed him with an unbridled sparkle of joy had smote him in an instant. *We talked for so long I missed class.*

Sam stood, placing the mug with care. He didn't want to make a sound.

God, her laugh. I kept telling stupid joke after stupid joke just to keep her laughing. I don't think I've ever seen a smile that's made me happier.

The world was still and silent. His feet made no noise on the tile. Nat seemed frozen in time, locked in place with that same smile as he reached the drawer. The smell of ash hung heavy in the kitchen air as he picked out a knife, a flood of memories flowing past his vision.

And then later that week. The first time she said "I love you." That first kiss under the streetlamp in the spring night.

He found the bucket, the bottom caked with ruddy dust. Armed with his tools he turned to face his partner, still lost in her own world. *If only there was time for one last embrace.*

"I love you, Nat." he whispered, holding back tears, his words dying in the air before they could make a sound.

Without another word he left the kitchen, leaving Nat with the immaculate sunrise.

***

Nat won't understand, but she'll be safe from me, Sam thought, walking with quiet purpose towards his fate. Resolve lay heavy in his stomach like lead. *The wall wants me, and it'll have me.* Within moments he was once more in front of the wall, its bland surface radiating terrible mirth. There was no hesitation as he set down the bucket and pressed the knife to his forearm, his teeth grinding together at the sting of his cut and the itching warmth of his blood against his skin.

"Have to work fast before I pass out," he whispered, wetting his finger with the blood before pressing it to the canvas before him, letting his flowing blood drip into the bucket (*the carpet's white, it would stain pretty badly*). Claustrophobia hit him at the heaviness of the still and silent air. The way his bloody finger traced the lines upon the wall felt routine as if he had done this hundreds of times. Sam spoke the words which the lines had whispered to him in the night.

"*Echlas, mnaig, chacthod, ledinedaer nachthleig.*"

They meant nothing and everything. Sam could not understand them no matter how many times the wall bade him repeat them, yet he could feel energy spark from the sounds they made as the words struck the air and latched onto the bloody lines. Each time he pressed his finger to the wall after refreshing its crimson ink, the wall hummed with greater exuberance. The eye, closed but alert, shuddered with sickening excitement as the lattice came closer to completion. Sam continued to draw, continued to chant. From somewhere in the distance, he heard the grinding agonized wail of the dead sun, sourceless and silent.

Within a matter of minutes he was done. Sam half expected a crash of thunder or a bray of sirens when his finger connected the last lines together. What he got instead was a silence more deafening than anything he could have imagined.

Dizziness hit him as blood loss began to take its toll. Preempting a collapse, he stumbled back to let the railing take his weight. Now realized, the lines on the wall seemed both chaotic and ordered, a maddening weave like the web of some deranged arachnid. In the center rested the eye. A mixture of fear and awe gripped him as it opened, its impossible pupil bathing him in ashy red shadow. Ever wider the eye opened, stretching to span the whole height of the wall. As in his vision before, those toothy fingers grew from the pupil, though now they pulled and stretched its dark depths to make space for their prey.

Sam couldn't count how many fingers he saw, not even as they stretched and cracked to wrap around his body and cradled him like a hammock made of skin, bone, and teeth. The fingers bit and tugged, digging into his flesh, dragging him towards the ashy world and the throng of hissing shadows. In his pain, Sam released a terrible howl, closing his eyes and conjuring an image of Nat in his mind one last time before his consciousness failed and he was cast into the ashy tundra of the corpse world and its cadaverous sun.

Again there was silence, alone upon the empty landing with nothing to hear it save a pristine, featureless wall.

***

Nat looked up from her phone. *Was that a shout?* She looked over to Sam only to find his seat empty.

"Sam? Where'd you go? Did you hear something?" she called, her voice harsh in her ears.

No answer. As the sun peeked over the fence heralding a beautiful day, a cold feeling bubbled into the base of her skull. *Something's not right,* muttered a thought in her head. With care she set her mug on the island, the click of the ceramic in sync with the scuffing squeak of her chair across the tile as she crept from the kitchen.

The sun hadn't had time to warm the house with its fresh morning light, and Nat shivered at the touch of the chill air which filled the dark hallway. Her nose wrinkled for a moment at a brief smell of ash which vanished before confusion could make a foothold in her mind.

Nat walked to the foot of the stairs, her slippers shuffling across the wood floor the only audible sound amidst the silence.

"Sam?" she called again, projecting her voice up the stairwell. For a moment, she strained her ears, listening for a response but again finding nothing. A weird feeling she couldn't quite describe hung wavy in the air: it reminded her of the static electricity before a strike of thunder, though the description wasn't quite right.

Something in her peripheral vision caught her attention. On instinct, her gaze darted to try and bring it into focus, but whatever she had seen was gone by the time her eyes rested upon the boring, beige wall on the landing.

In the five odd years they had lived in the same house, Nat had never noticed the wall.

It was one of those surreal recognitions: that first acknowledgment of something you've walked past innumerable times but never given a moment's thought. One of those things that you never cease to notice once you're aware of it.

"Huh," huffed Nat, confused at why her attention was drawn to the wall's plain, unadorned surface.

Without any thought, she climbed the stairs to get a closer look, the thoughts of screams and of Sam lost to the fog of coffee and her newfound curiosity.

Something had caught her attention, and she really needed to see it.

WHITE NOISE

He cleaned his dishes.

After a long day glued to his phone, the back of his throat the consistency of sandpaper from hours of phone calls, he relished the opportunity for contemplation.

The warmth of the soapy water soaked into his hands as he worked through the pile of dirty plates and utensils in his sink, the heat soothing ingrained tension in his arms. His chest swelled with deep breaths of humid air scented with marinara and beef fat as he leaned into the comfortable blanket of white noise that enveloped him: the convivial hum of kitchen appliances, chattering amongst themselves with enthusiasm; the gentle scrape of his sponge against damp ceramic; the sheet of sound that rippled from the running tap; the crash of waves of wind through the trees outside his small apartment.

Despite the soreness at the back of his throat, a spontaneous hum of contentment escaped his lips. Thoughts fluttered through his consciousness: moths drawn to the light of indecision over what to do once the dishes were finished.

His listless gaze gravitated towards the off-white orb of the streetlamp outside, only just visible between the half-shuttered blinds as it flickered in the thrashing shadows of the leaves.

A show or a movie might be good, mused a thought, absent of enthusiasm, crushed by the burden of having to choose something from the long list of friends' recommendations. *Maybe a book, or ...*

The heavy, erratic buzz of a fly derailed his train of thought. Fresh agitation festered behind his brow as its unpredictable *thuds* against the window stuck in his ears, keeping his attention fixated on when next it would hit the glass. He gave the window a glare, his eyes darting across the pane. But against the darkness of the night, he could not catch signs of movement.

Hoping to push the sound out of his attention, he doubled down on the dishes, focusing his annoyance into scraping charred meat and tomato off of the bottom of his cast iron pan. As if released by his distraction, uncomfortable thoughts resurfaced in his head. His mind returned to the conversation from earlier that had laid simmering, a cocktail of guilt and discomfort in its tow.

"Have you seen Sarah?"

The tear-drenched words echoed in his memory, the image of Matt's red eyes and damp cheeks so vivid that he swore he felt their gaze boring into him. He remembered how the silence had closed around the two of them in that moment, how heavy it had felt, how thirsty for sorrow.

"She went for a walk last night in the evening, and ... I've been trying to text her all day but nothing is going through. Has she messaged you or anything?"

"I'm really sorry, I haven't been in touch with her. I'll let you know if I do hear anything."

His response echoed in his mind, his thoughts turning over the empty sympathy of it. *Surely, there was more you could have said or done.*

More flies added themselves to the hubbub at the window, drawing him back to the present. He stopped his scrubbing, craning his neck to try and catch sight of movement. The droning menagerie bashed themselves against the glass with a violent fervor that got under his skin. Despite his craning, despite his staring, he could see no sign of them.

More flies, more and more, their tempo picking up. In his ear, the sound was far too close to the sound of someone tapping long nails on the outside of the window. He let the pan drop, shuddering at the grating *crunch* it made against the sedimentary layer of crumbs that coated the metal sink.

In one swift motion, he pulled the blinds open, a medley of frustration and confusion boiling over in his mind as he scanned the corners of the window for the sudden swarm of insects.

Still, no physical sign of flies. Only the accelerating cacophony of fearful buzzing and taping against the glass. He took a step back from the sink, the hiss of water from the faucet taking on a new, unsettling timbre. The tapping against the window turned to visible shaking. He froze, confusion paralyzing him. A rhythm appeared from within the din: three heavy strikes against the glass that repeated over the chaotic rumbling of the window. A familiar rhythm, the cadence of a voice. In the depths of the unrelenting rhythm, he swore he heard screaming.

"Let me in, let me in!"

In the moment, fear overriding his thoughts, he inched back to the sink. Only now did he see them: two pale fists in the dark, hammering upon the outside of his window. In the shadow of the night, the haggard contour of Sarah's face faded in and out of view, a faint glow of fear in her eyes.

"Let me in, let me in!"

Panic consumed him, his own surprise and terror leaping up his throat. Not thinking, forgetting that he was on the second floor, he flung the window open. The screech of rusted metal joined the hum of flies and pounding of flesh against glass, piercing his ears as the sharp night air cut against his cheeks.

And then silence.

A profound, overwhelming silence, all consuming. He stood, confusion needling at his brain as he stared outside.

A new sound intruded: a low, humming drone. The sound of a distant swarm.

At once, it sunk into his skull, the auditory equivalent of a ghost stain on a white shirt, only visible to someone who knows where to look.

"The hell is that?" he muttered, turning off the tap to get a better grasp of the sound.

With the viscosity of oil, the low buzz filled the space once occupied by the sound of running water. His ears told him the sound grew louder. *Not louder, deeper.* The more space the sound occupied, the more it flowered, the more profound, distinct details he could hear within. Fear at the back of his raw throat, he paced the kitchen, seeking the sound's source as his ears absorbed the manifold depths of the intrusive sound. He thought he heard a voice lurking within the web of sound: a soft, gentle, welcoming voice that seemed pleased to find ears to fall upon.

"Come to us."

The words fluttered against the inside of his skull, moths of sound buffeting against the light of his thoughts. *That voice...* His gaze once more settled on the orb of light outside his window, on the sharp shadows it cast against the trees writing in the wind, catching the moment something large and amorphous moved before it.

Terror overpowered him at the smothering of the light. He dashed from the kitchen into the living room, the need to drown out the drone with loud music or an explosive movie burning in his mind. His nose burned as he inhaled the cold air, the crisp, green scent of frost on spring leaves rushing into his nostrils.

"How ... " he muttered, vertigo tugging at his head. The empty street stretched before him, the light of the streetlamp catching against the gritty surface of unkempt asphalt and egregious potholes. He turned, looked up, his heart dropping as his eyes caught the light from his apartment window above him.

The wind stilled as he stared in disbelief, the heavy drone rolling against his back, digging into his muscles. Static prickled the hairs on the back of his neck, his eyes descending to stare at his elongated shadow in the light. Fresh terror clawed at his throat as he noticed a second human shadow merging with his.

Once more he turned, and felt his jaw drop.

It hovered before him. A narrow, vertical ellipse haloed in white light, a few meters above the ground. A film of static bubbled around its circumference, the space within its dark mass swarming with undulating masses of insects' wings. Awe washed across his mind, his head buzzing, his eyes darting across its dark surface, not sure where to focus. Human hands drifted half-seen within the shadowed mass. Strange faces, too gaunt, too long to be human, pressed through the film of shadow as though rising out of water, delight etched into their winged mouths.

Terror coursed through his heart, yet also a sense of ... joy? Exultation? The buzzing in his head, a thick drone as if bees had gotten into his skull, made it hard to grasp what he felt.

"Do not be afraid," it said, its voice a balm in his ear against the harsh buzz. "Come, join us."

A cry for help tried to escape his gaping mouth but found itself deafened, a buzz vibrating the inside of his cheeks, pins and needles sending waves of static through his mouth. Confusion, fear, and nausea churned in his stomach, his tongue testing sharp, vibrating growths poking from the backs of his teeth. His knees buckled, that sense of nausea overpowering his will, his stomach relinquishing its contents. Thick, red streaked chunks of matter spilled from his mouth, twitching dragonfly wings sprouting from many small, dark holes across their slick surfaces. Blunt surprise blanketed his mind as he watched his vomit take flight to join the cloud before him.

"Come, join us," the voice said once more, its kindness jarring against the searing pain in his arms. He stared in dismay at the countless pits growing across his skin, squirming with sharp things trying to escape and take flight. Fuzzy spots spread across his vision, an uncomfortable pull tugging at his eyes as insectoid wings pushed their way out of his pupils and tickled at the insides of his sockets.

He screamed, one final agonized, terrified scream, a thick stream of sharp wings billowing from his throat before his consciousness failed him, his body evaporating into a droning mist.

And then silence.

Mourning

The path stretched before her, its dusty surface a wound carved into the sullen, wild grass. The question of where she was had dissolved into the briny morass of her twisting thoughts hours ago, the oppressiveness of the fog in her head in sync with the dreary, sunless sky above. Soft hills came and went around her path, rolling waves of green stretching to the gray horizon. Occasional mounds, crowned with weathered stones and stunted, tired trees, punctuated the empty landscape. Beyond that, there was nothing save grass and its secretive whispers.

She continued on her path. Her nose wrinkled with a gust of frigid air. A slick, greasy scent of motor oil tried to force its way into her nostrils: the first smell she could recall experiencing in hours. The faintest of cries buffeted her ears, an all too human sob just audible above the whistle of the grass. Anxiety settled its electric web over the top of her mind, certainty that something awaited beyond the top of the next mound setting down roots.

For a moment, she considered turning back, a sickening pit forming in her stomach as her legs continued to move forward without her input. In her head, a silent, wordless thought floated into her consciousness: a need to witness the source of the cries. The notion that the thought did not originate in her mind only added the well-fueled engine of fear purring in her chest.

Mercy allowed the object of her anxiety to be brief. Cresting one last, small hill a vague shadow on the road caught her eye, swaying back and forth with the rhythmic accuracy of a pendulum. At a distance, she could pick out the contours of an emaciated, kneeling human frame, their face resting in their bony hands. Fear gave way to morbid curiosity as she approached, the figure's ceaseless wailing catching in her ears with hooks of pity. That this person mourned over something she had no doubt, and so she allowed herself to walk faster until she stood only a few paces away.

The kneeled figure rocked before her, their agony a flower, a beacon of emotion in the bleak world around them. Little remained of their clothes, or their flesh: only ancient remnants spared from the wastes of time by mere luck, held together by fragments of the heartiest threads and tenacious strands of sinew. And grief. Some odd, dream-logic sense of intuition told her that grief alone remained of whatever person they had once been.

She watched over their mourning. Watched as the corpse rocked and wailed over some pile of dust, punctuated with scraps of cloth. Winces danced across her lips with each hoarse scream of grief that filled the space, the coarse sound driven into her bones with the cold, uncaring relentlessness of iron nails hammered by an unpracticed hand. Despite the cries of pain, she found herself without tears to shed. Guilt made its home in her lungs, guilt that her emotions had become as empty as the landscape around them. At the same time, a sense of release grew within her, another wordless feeling that perhaps being witness to this long dead person's mourning was all they needed.

With that thought in her head, she planted herself next to the kneeled figure, warm pain stabbing at her legs from the path's loose stones. Tentative at first, she reached her arm around the rocking figure, resisting the urge to recoil at the cold, coarse texture of their ruined body. No words found their way to her lips, no empathetic condolences or affirmations: just silence. The figure sobbed on, their overwhelming grief now accompanied by an odd, warm sense of gratitude.

She watched over their mourning, held them, projected her condolences until the figure ground themself to dust upon the coarse path, joining whatever they had been mourning over. And once nothing was left, she moved on, soles crunching against the rocky, dusty path: wondering if she, too, would weather herself into dust walking its infinite expanse.

Joanne's Vault

The harsh buzz of the doorbell wrenched Joanne from the depths of sleep.

Darkness of the night replaced the darkness of her dreamless rest as her eyelids snapped open. For a brief moment, a spark of panic flared in her mind: panic that she had missed her alarm, panic that her transformation was imminent. She hadn't prepared. There was no time to get to the basement, to fasten the chains and take the sedatives. Nothing was in place to stop her from getting out and …

She caught the train of thought before it drove too far out of her grasp. "It wasn't the alarm," she whispered to herself, her heart pounding. "You don't need the alarm any more, remember? It's bound in the tattoos. You are in control. Everything is fine." Joanne took a deep breath, allowing the heavy lightness that comes with meditation to wash through her body. A tingling, wriggling sensation rippled through the tattoos on her arms, reminding her of their presence. The feeling sent shivers across her body but also provided a sense of comfort. She was in control. There would be no more transformations.

Lying on her back, Joanne stared upwards into the abyss, hoping the doorbell had been conjured by her dreams in some attempt at a twisted joke. It took only moments for that hope to crumble, however, the bell emitting another horrid screech. What fragments of sleep remained evaporated from the surface of her mind, replaced by seething annoyance. On instinct, Joanne reached for her phone on the bedside table to check the time. "4:17 a.m," read the lock screen, the glaring white numbers almost exuding a sense of mockery. *Do people not fucking sleep,* asked an incredulous voice in her head. In the comfort of the dark, the warm embrace of her blankets shielding her from the chill of the outside world, she found little impetus to placate the person disturbing her slumber: whoever was at the door could wait there all week for all she cared.

As if the visitor had heard her thought, the doorbell buzzed yet again, the electric clamor tearing at her place of comfort. *Someday I'm going to rip out that buzzer and just let them push the damn button till their fingers fall off,* growled Joanne's internal monologue. Another series of buzzes fired off, only intensifying her desire to make that thought a reality. She rolled onto her side to get some light, her teeth clenching at the stiffness in her back. Dim, amber light splashed against the drab, wood walls of her studio with the soft click of the lamp chain, a grimace dancing across her lips as her eyes adjusted. Knowing another unnecessary buzz was inevitable, Joanne pushed herself up to a sitting position with a guttural sigh. With practiced efficiency she got dressed, rifling through the pile of clothes on the ground for the most convenient pair of jeans and a t-shirt to go over her camisole.

"What kind of *fun* awaits us this time," she muttered under her breath, her words sharp enough to draw blood as she shoved on heavy boots. Fueled by agitation, her mind dredged up her previous encounters with post-midnight callers, tormenting her with half-remembered, infuriating conversations.

Despite her best efforts, word of the vault had escaped into the wider world, luring would-be wizards and magic practitioners out of the woodwork seeking easy acquisitions. Every month it felt like there were more of them: insufferable, entitled asshats rocking up to the door long before the sun was due, a demand for access to the vault and its contents on their lips. "This isn't a fucking pawnshop for your deranged rituals," she rehearsed her usual line, playing with how coarse she could get her voice to sound without getting that scratching feeling in her throat.

Joanne flipped through her phone, dragging the heels of her boots across the hardwood floor and shuffling over to the kitchenette in the front right corner of the studio apartment. Beyond the endless morass of spam and scams, the only message of importance she could find was a text from Melissa to schedule another appointment. "Be more like Melissa; make damn appointments when the sun's out, dipshits," she grumbled under her breath, making a mental note to respond at a more reasonable hour. Eyes still on her phone she plunged her hand into the sink, exhuming a serviceable mug from the heap of uncleaned dishes before flipping the switch on the percolator. The image of the ring of burns around Melissa's neck snuck into her head as the acidic, ashy smell of old coffee hit her nose. Joanne had inked over uncountable scars without a passing thought, but something about Melissa's burns put her on edge. She wasn't sure if it was the way you could see the imprints of the hot nails in her skin or if it was the story she had told of how she earned the scars.

No one should have to go through that, mourned a thought, not for the first time. *She didn't deserve it, her daughter ...what's-her-face ... didn't deserve it.* A trace of guilt ran through Joanne's head as she loomed over the coffee machine, her brain reveling in a descent towards rumination. How often had Melissa brought her along to check up on objects in the vault? How often had she told the girl not to touch anything with a harsh word?

The kid brought you flowers and made you cookies after Erica told her you were "sick," and yet you can't remember her name. "Plenty of time to think about it later," Joanne bemoaned with a tinge of sarcasm. Shaking her head to fling the thoughts away she grabbed the creamer from the fridge, hoping it might give her coffee the illusion of potability.

Not even a sip passed her lips before the doorbell buzzed *yet again*: a long, drawn out screech as the person at the door held their finger on the button. "OK, ok, Jesus Christ I'm coming!" Joanne yelled in no direction in particular, not to alert the people at the door but rather to just enjoy being loud for a moment. Clenching her nose, she downed as much coffee as she could without burning her tongue. She gave the studio a cursory glance, in part to tick off boxes in her mental checklist but more so to stall a little longer: *keys, wallet, phone ... check. Alright, let's get this over with.* With a clatter, she unfastened the chain lock and turned the deadbolt. The door required a hearty tug to wrench open, and Joanne was more than happy to release some pent up frustration on that task. As her boots crunched against the firm carpeted floor of the stairwell, the desire to stall tugged at her.

The feeling was cut short by an abrupt sense of unease that draped itself over Joanne's shoulders with the harsh slam of her studio door behind her. An unexpected tension settled in her lungs, constricting her breath. Paranoia tickled the nape of her neck with its sharp, chilling fingers, seizing and jerking her senses around the hall to identify the unseen danger. In a glance, she found only familiarity. The narrow passage harbored its usual, moody yellow illumination. The familiar drone of the ancient building's struggling central heating unit and the hallway's failing light bulbs beat against her eardrums. From the carpet wafted the ashy, briny smell of cigarette smoke and dust and road salt. It was an unpleasant atmosphere, yes. But it was a familiar, acceptable kind of unpleasant: the kind of unpleasantness that has nothing to hide. Yet still, the unease nagged at her.

A squirming sensation drove her to look down at her arms, a prickling feeling of concern blossoming at the base of her skull as she pushed against the cloud of unease between her and the foot of the stairs. Ethereal, blue-green sparks danced along the intricate black runes and interlocking circles of her inked sleeves, her skin trying to retreat into the flesh below at the light's oily, electric touch. *Something dangerous ahead,* muttered a thought in her head, a thought in a voice she had never heard yet could still identify: the voice of the thing trapped in her tattoos. Joanne wrung her arms out in an attempt to fling away the feeling.

It's getting stronger, murmured another thought, worrying a divot into her mind.

Erica had predicted that the entity responsible for Joanne's transformations wouldn't stay quiet forever. "It was weak when we trapped it," she had warned, "Sooner or later there's gonna be more energy stuck in those wards than your body can handle. Like it or not, you're gonna have to work with that thing in there someday."

Maybe tonight will be that 'sooner or later,' she mused in her head, uncomfortable at the excitement the thought elicited. Continuing her descent to the base of the stairs, she could not shake loose a primal sense that conflict was nigh. After what felt like half an hour, she reached the door and, creeping up to the peephole, she pressed her face against the fishbowl lens to see what was waiting for her.

Three people stood beyond the door, trapped in a globe of yellow light from the streetlamp beyond which there was nothing but darkness. Age had yet to weather what she could see of their faces: the lines that did dwell upon them were lines of anxiety and fear alone. The way they huddled close to each other, shying from the boundaries of the light, stirred up a dust storm of pity and guilt in Joanne's mind.

All those complaints and you were just making scared kids wait in the dark. Her tattoos quivered again, saving her from any further rumination. Awareness of an odd feeling of cold emanating from the people outside settled in her head. With an unnerving exactness, the sensation reminded her of the feeling of being around the dead: of the profound, lifeless silence that wanders forests of granite headstones; of the heaviness of the air, weighed down by the awareness of one's own mortality; of the feeling that something is using the wind to whisper into your ear, inviting you to contemplate the grave. A shiver radiated from her core. For a moment, Joanne swore her heart had frozen from the chill of the atmosphere of death. Crawling into her ear, she heard whispers from below her feet: voices inviting her to lie down and let herself pass into the unknown, white hot fear piercing her gut as she realized she had in fact started to lie down without noticing.

Ok, first and foremost, fuck whatever that is, shouted her inner monologue. Erica and Melissa had brought plenty of things for her to store in the vault: magical objects wrenched from sites of **Power** (emphasis and capitalization required); occult foci, talismans, and wards crafted with materials ranging from the mundane to the macabre; failed experiments (and successful ones), forged in the hopes of discovering more about the lengths to which magic could be utilized. Plenty of the things in the vault were awful, but certainty dug its stubborn heels into Joanne's head that the thing beyond the door got the grand prize.

Nothing down there feels as wrong as this.

They probably don't know you heard the bell, whispered a compelling thought in her head. *Hell, they might think you're not home, or that they've got the wrong place. Maybe they didn't hear you yell from upstairs. You could let them leave, let them take whatever ... whoever has those bad vibes as far from here as possible. There's nothing good that can come from something that feels like that.*

Just don't make a noise, wait for them to go away.

That's messed up and you know it, she rebuked. The group shuffled in the light as she debated, their movements almost in sync, taking turns to look behind them into the void of the night. *People didn't leave me alone and afraid when we were in a bad place. These kids need help, and whatever is giving off that energy belongs in the vault.*

It's a bad idea, I'm calling it, remarked the intrusive thought with a wry tone before crawling back into her subconscious. Her debate over, Joanne took a deep breath and opened the door with a tactical lack of grace.

"What do you want?" she barked at the small group, doing her best to hide her own anxiety behind a cloak of rancor. The visitors almost jumped at the sound of her voice as it pierced the stillness of the night. With the door no longer between them, the smell of blood struck her nose, the scent hanging around them like a strong cloud of cologne. Repugnance gnawed at Joanne's mind with how fast she could pick out that smell. The sweet, rusty scent made her salivate, made her stomach groan with hunger. Even with the wards on her arms, she could feel her muscles crawling, wanting to change. She could feel the raging desire to seek out the thrill of the hunt, to claim its reward of raw flesh. But with another deep breath between her teeth she quelled those feelings. She was in control. There would be no change.

With pronounced hesitation, the young man at the head of the party stepped forward, shielding his eyes from the light as he looked up to meet her gaze.

"Uh, hi. Sorry to bother you at this time of night. My name is Alex." Alex cleared his throat before turning to the people behind him. "That over there is Dave," he continued, pointing to the man to his right, "and over there in the hoodie is Morgan." Morgan cracked a nervous, awkward smile with their introduction, their heavy, blood spattered hoodie concealing most of their face. Alex cleared his throat again, "We were, uh, told that we should come to this address with this ... thing."

The *thing* rested in Morgan's arms. Swaddled with some sort of rough cloth the object looked innocuous, little more than an amorphous bundle the size of a small dog. Joanne squinted to try and get a better sense of the shape and size of the swaddled thing but found no better details. Light recoiled from its surface, casting it in perfect shadow. In one blink of an eye, it was motionless and at the same time shifted and crawled. The chill of the grave pulsed from it, rippled through the air, leaving in its wake the scent of wet stone and rich earth and the silent wails of grieving mothers. Without the door to act as a barrier, the presence of death was overwhelming. She wondered for a moment if the three before her felt it as much as she.

Joanne did her best to not look concerned. "Ok, so you have this ... thing. *Who* was it that said you should come here?"

The three looked at each other, their shoulders tightening in unified panic before Alex turned back to give her an answer.

"It was this FBI guy, Lucas. Lucas Blake, I think. He said that, uh, this thing we found ... that we should take it to someone named Joanne, so she and some other people could put it in some sort of vault. Are you Joanne?"

Joanne chewed at her inner lip to hide her frustration. *Would it kill that fucker to give people some forewarning?* She looked beyond the small group into the dark of the empty street, her eyes jumping along the vibrant circles of light cast upon the sidewalk at regular intervals as far as her vision traveled. A visceral, primal instinct bubbled into consciousness in the back of her head: a feeling of certainty that something lurked in the far dark. Something predatory. Again, the regret of stalling so long hit her, but she knew the time had passed to dwell on that. It was time to act.

"Yes, that's me," she said in the calmest voice she could muster, closing the door behind her and locking up. "If Lucas sent you it must be important. Come with me, and hurry. We'll talk when we're in the vault."

The door to the tattoo parlor was just six feet to the right: a convenient commute in normal circumstances. Tonight, however, the overwhelming darkness around them brought her a sense of vulnerability. An almost human whisper of the wind fluttered past Joanne's ears, a sense of fear precipitating from the air itself as if it was fleeing something in terror. Fumbling in the dark with her keys, Joanne found herself thankful that Erica had convinced her to paint wards along the borders of her windows: intricate, weaving bands of runes which gave off a vague hum in the silence. In a way, it reminded Joanne of the sound you got by running a finger around the rim of a crystal wine glass. *Hopefully, the runes buy some time,* she mused, a fragment of relief chipping at her anxiety as the key found its place in the lock. With a quick pull, she wrenched the glass door open, funneling Alex, Dave, and Morgan inside. Taking one last survey of the street, Joanne ducked in after them, closing the door as fast as possible, the fear of the unseen snapping at her heels.

***

"Alright, move quickly. The vault's this way."

Joanne found herself whispering as she fastened the deadbolt with a deafening *click,* the fear that something might be listening grasping at the back of her mind. A strong gust of wind jostled at the door as soon as her hand left the handle, catching her off guard and sucking the breath from her lungs. Lunging away from the shuddering glass, she thought she heard voices in the wind, weeping in fear, begging to be let in. Light from the streetlamp outside shone through the windows, weak and pale, emitting only a narrow bar of illumination for the first few feet of the store. Upon the weathered hardwood floors, the shadows cast from the runes on her window gave off the eerie impression of movement, arcs of half-seen energy fluttering around their serpentine curves. Joanne did not tarry long looking at the runes: the longer she stared the more they reminded her of unknown things slithering below the surface of water. Instead, she turned to face the back wall, fumbling for her phone, turning on the flashlight and casting away the darkness in a small circle before her.

For half a decade, Joanne had worked in this storefront: first as a fledgling artist, now as an owner. It was her second home. *Hell, the apartment is more like the second home given how much time I spend there,* she corrected. Oftentimes after long days, she found peace within the darkness of the store once the lights were out, within the silence that came after the clients were gone and the tools had ceased their aggressive droning, in just picking a chair and watching life pass by her storefront. But tonight, her shop possessed an unsettling mockery of its usual familiarity. There was no visible difference to the darkness or the silence if she directed her senses to them. Yet despite what her senses told her, the feeling of comfort and the tranquility of night felt shattered by the deathly presence she had allowed to enter, twisted into a morass of dread.

Joanne padded towards the back of the room. With each footfall, she swore she heard dead leaves crunching under her boots. Shadows skittered from the light her phone cast: half-seen shapes, bodiless things with many jagged limbs, crawling to hide under the sturdy chairs upon which her clients were inked. The photos taped to the walls, sketches of common tattoo choices and examples of her past projects, glowered in places with an uncanny similarity to the reflection of cats' eyes in the dark. In the air hung a vague, sourceless scent of moss, earth, and wet stone.

Joanne looked back towards the window. Alex, Dave, and Morgan stood huddled in the nook to her left, pressing themselves against the plastic chairs reserved for waiting clients. From the stunned looks on their faces, Joanne suspected they were experiencing shock from whatever they must have witnessed. *You can sympathize with that, can't you,* scoffed a voice in her head with bottomless self repugnance and guilt. The click of an unlocking door reverberated in her brain as horrible memories flung themselves into the forefront of her consciousness: memories of waking in the woods, skin burst in strips along her limbs, her raw, stinging muscles encrusted with coarse dirt and leaf fragments; memories of the feeling of someone's fragmented bones caught in the roof of her mouth, the lingering taste of flesh and fat and blood on her tongue; memories of confusion as she lay curled up in a ball, unsure of where or who she was, surrounded by the remains of half eaten friends that stared at her with lifeless, judgmental eyes.

Again, the wind tried the door, all too human screams of panic rattling the glass and snapping Joanne back to the present. A fresh chill blossomed deep in her bones, her skin crawling at the feeling of her tattoos squirming into her flesh: *Something's coming. We need to stop stalling and get into the vault. The window's aren't going to hold.* The sound of breaking glass conjured itself into her mind at the thought. Looking beyond the window into the street, certain something horrible would appear at any moment, Joanne shook away the last fragments of introspection and cleared her throat.

"Come on, you heard me, let's go!" she growled, beckoning with her hand towards the back of the store, unsure of how long she had stood trapped among her memories. Snapped out of their own trances, Alex, Dave, and Morgan nodded, forming up like ducklings after their mother as Joanne forged a path through the darkness.

They made up for wasted time. Within a matter of paces, the four of them crossed the store and crowded into the rectangular alcove in the back left of the room. The stairs descended parallel to the front of the store, blocking her line of sight to the window. As soon as Joanne was convinced they were all out of sight from the window, she flicked the lightswitch and closed the basement door, the warmth of the light providing a soothing moment of respite from the dread. Creaks and groans from the old wood stairs accompanied their descent, the familiar sounds a welcome distraction to the doom-drenched ambiance provided by the object among them.

A modest, well-lit rectangle of a room greeted them at the bottom of the stairs, unadorned save for a few shelves full of boxes and a desk inundated with unsorted forms and bills. For once, Joanne found a semblance of comfort and security in the plainness of the room. For once, she was glad she hadn't chosen to do more than tidy up the cracks and chips in the drab white paint: nothing malign could hide within walls so boring and featureless. Moving with purpose, she made her way to the back right corner from the stairs, moving a prop shelf aside to reveal a concealed entrance to the v ault.

On occasion, the thought arose in Joanne's mind that fate had some hand in the vault's existence. The thought was one she was quick to dismiss. Even considering the notion that her pain served a greater purpose filled her stomach with a nauseating sense of injustice. The pain of the families she had destroyed, their mangled loved ones lying buried in unmarked graves deep in the woods of Massachusetts, only added to her distaste for the idea that this was all just "one big plan." Melissa and Erica had discovered the vault while cleaning up "leftovers" from one of Joanne's transformations. Joanne remembered watching them, holding herself in a tight ball in the nook under the stairs: she remembered the bizarre feeling of seeing that hole dug through the solid concrete floor, knowing that she had carved through it with her own fingers. Even now it terrified her to think that, while transformed, some instinct had driven her to burrow after returning with a kill, leaving her fingers splintered after she once more assumed control. Sunrise had hit before the hole was wide enough to pass through, but what had her possessor been planning to do with the chamber it had uncovered?

That was almost a year and a half ago, Joanne ruminated, her eyes gravitating towards the phantom remains of the bloodstains on the floor that no amount of scrubbing seemed to be able to erase. Despite the passage of time, sparks of pain lanced through her fingertips when she looked upon the rectangular, iron trapdoor that now covered the rough passage. With idle, practiced movements she reached for the trapdoor handle, catching herself and stopping her arm with a jerking half-recoil moments before touching the dark steel. "Shit," she muttered, unaware that she cursed out loud.

How many times have you made a fool of yourself forgetting the wards on the door, said a demeaning voice in her head.

At least twice, she responded, cringing at memories of flashing an awkward smile at Erica while she tugged at the unresponsive door.

Though it was subtle, Joanne caught angry, yellow flashes arcing through the intricate lattice of protection runes when she focused her sight: a sign the wards upon the door were in fact active. She cleared her throat, whispering in the shy hope that her guests wouldn't hear.

"Uhh, ***Ehedran!***"

Heat filled her cheeks as they flushed with embarrassment, as it did every time she had to work magic in front of people. At the same time, Joanne got a shot of thrill at the heaviness of the word on her tongue, at the raw feeling of **Power** that passed through her lips. She paused to give the enchantment a chance to work, satisfaction kicking in when the door opened with a hefty tug.

By reflex, Joanne wrinkled her nose as her head got below door level. Even after months of cleaning, a sweet and tangy scent of expired wine lingered in the still, humid atmosphere.

"***Malchatar!***" she shouted, her teeth buzzing at the force of the word as it pushed through the thick air. With a flash, a dozen sconces sprung to life with ethereal, yellow flames, filling the room with soft light, motes of fire fluttering to the arched ceiling like vibrant butterflies before fading into nothingness. A smile snuck onto Joanne's face upon hearing a whispered "whoa" from behind.

Melissa speculated that the sub basement must have been built at some point during Prohibition: a covert winery and speakeasy, built in secret and then sealed away to avoid trouble after secrecy was no longer needed. The furniture they had found on their first expedition had been enough to give the theory credence, from the long oak wood bar to the dozen rotting tables and chairs: time had reduced most of it to little more than splinters and sawdust held together by mold, but Joanne had salvaged what she could. Four large, half-cylinder alcoves comprised the wall to the right of the stairs.

In each were stuffed shelves fashioned from what planks seemed fit to bear weight, recycled from the old barrels that had once lived there. Though the sub basement was huge, the shelves and tables were already stacked high with parcels, jars, random junk, and overstuffed notebooks. Magic coursed through all of them in one way or another, filling the room with a buzz of energy similar to the dull whine of an electrical substation.

"Ok, go ahead and set it there," Joanne said to no one in particular, pointing at a heavy, rectangular oak table near the center. Free of clutter and inscribed with its own runes, it was the designated "observation table," the go-to place to inspect new entries to the vault. "And take a seat," she added, "You all look like you could use a rest."

From the nook under the stairs, she produced three folding chairs, setting them along the table. Alex, Dave, and

Morgan shuffled around the chairs a moment, evoking the image of seagulls circling a promising morsel before sitting down one by one. Morgan sat down last, placing the morbid, bundled object upon the table before sitting with a profound expression of relief.

Joanne nodded to indicate satisfaction before circling around the table to get a better look at the bundle. Even in the presence of magical light, it accepted no illumination, the flatness of the shadows making it appear two dimensional, a cutout of darkness in three dimensional space. Though the room was filled with the white noise of a myriad of magical sources, each chiming and humming at their own tune, the bundle's morbid aura overpowered them all. *I don't think I should touch this thing before I give the coven a call,* muttered Joanne's internal monologue, even as the desire to feel its texture upon her fingers snuck into her mind. *One curse per lifetime is enough for me.* Looking over to Morgan, their angular, androgynous face nested within the darkness of their hoodie, Joanne wondered whether a curse now sat upon their shoulders. *Why is it always the people who are unaware of magic that get the worst of it thrust upon them?*

Joanne threw a question into the sour air. In part, she asked out of necessity, but in reality the question was designed to kill the unbearable silence.

"So ... " The awkwardness of the word seemed to hang in the air like an unpleasant smell. "Where did you find this thing?"

From the way they squirmed in their chairs and looked at their feet, Joanne gathered they were uncomfortable with the question. *Good talk,* berated her internal monologue. "Sorry, that was a stupid question," she added, floundering for the right words to rescue what felt like a doomed conversation.

"If it helps at all, I've been in your shoes. Sort of." She could almost hear the sound of a shovel striking earth as she dug a deeper hole for herself, but she continued, "Got sort of this ... curse ... thing that I got a while back. You know, like a werewolf sort of curse except I don't think I turn into a wolf. No one has really told me what I turn into, just that I've ... done a lot of really bad things when I've turned. So, whatever you've seen, I get it. If that helps at all, or anything."

The viscosity of the awkwardness in the air only intensified.

"Can I get you all some coffee, or like a ..."

"No, no, it's fine, really!" replied Alex in a tone somewhere between apologetic and agitated, his words punctuated by the incessant tapping of his right foot. "Thanks for the words and, you know, letting us in. I really just don't know where to start."

"Benny got loose when we were at a park in Westmoore and ran after something in the woods," Dave blurted out, his soft baritone voice filling the silence. The words fell out of his mouth in a clip as though he had been waiting for a moment to let everything out all evening. *Westmoore. Again?* A vague sense of dreadful recognition tried to ignite itself in the back of Joanne's mind but found itself lacking fuel. *Lucas mentioned he had a lead on something over there a week ago, didn't he? What was it again?*

Joanne started searching for Westmoore on her phone, cursing at the signal strength down this deep underground while Dave continued his story.

"We ... we tried to catch him but the brush was really thick up there, and we couldn't get through it as fast as he could. He was barking at something. Like, we thought it had to be a squirrel. But then he cried out and went silent and ..." Joanne could hear his voice faltering, catching that wobbling, cracking tone of someone desperate to keep talking while holding back overwhelming emotions.

Alex seemed to pick up on it as well, wringing his hands as he took over the role of storyteller:

"It—that thing on the table—was just sitting on this sort of pedestal made from cinder blocks in the woods, and Benny was there staring at it when we got there, sort of half-growling and half-whimpering. I thought maybe the thing was just something somebody had set up as a joke. Just a weird, out of place thing to freak people out, you know? But when we got closer, there were bones sticking out of piles of leaves around the pedestal. Dave thought they looked human, but there weren't any skulls or rib cages or clothes, or anything like that so we weren't really sure. When we tried to pull Benny away, he got spooked and ran off deeper into the woods ..."

"There was something wrong about everything," added Morgan. Their voice was ethereal, muffled, almost silent as they sat motionless and stared at the concrete around their sneakers. "I heard dead people buried under the leaves, saying they were lonely and wanted us to lie there with them. One minute they were talking, and then that ... was in my hands, and I heard Alex asking me what was going on. I don't know why I picked it up."

"It was weird," said Alex, "like Morgan was sleepwalking or, you know, something like that. And then they picked it up and looked at us all confused and out of it, and told us about the dead people in the leaves so we looked and ..."

Alex fell silent, but the distance in his gaze told Joanne enough about what they had uncovered. By the time she looked at her phone, its screen glowed with the harsh white light of the search results page. An awful shudder wracked her body as she scrolled through the familiar headlines:

'*String of Suspected Suicides in Westmoore Continues, Bodies Still Missing;*'

'*19 Plots Excavated, Emptied Overnight in Westmoore Cemetery;*'

'*Keep Your Pets Indoors, Wild Animal Attacks on the Rise Around Westmoore!*'

"One of them was ... we knew him from college. He was still, you know ... warm, when we got all the leaves off," continued Alex. The words poured from his mouth like he was racing to get them out before they were drowned in tears. "It was only when we saw him and, you know, all the blood, that we realized there was blood in the brambles we were walking through. Got all over us. We thought maybe we could carry him out with us, call the cops or something. But we dropped him when Morgan screamed and started running ..."

"There was something in the woods," Morgan blurted out, lifting their head just enough for Joanne to see glossy lines on their face. "It ... it was as big as the trees. I didn't see its face but it looked like it was made of sticks, all broken and cracked out of shape. It saw me with this thing and it was mad, and when I screamed it started crawling through the bushes and ..." Morgan erupted into a fit of sob, burying their head into the bloody sleeves of their hoodie.

Joanne could not find any sympathetic words. Rummaging around her brain, her heart burdened with guilt at her own inability to provide comfort, every sentence she conjured felt like little more than a pathetic, throwaway consolation. In the end, she found enough words to cobble something together, understanding that something was better than nothing.

"But you got away, and with that bundle no less," she verbalized, hoping her tone was kind. "That's good. I think you might have stopped a whole lot more people dying." *I hope that's true.* "You met Lucas sometime after that?"

"Yeah," replied Dave, his weary face panning between her and Morgan. "He dropped by the house before we could call the cops. Said he was a fed looking for those people that went missing. Don't know how he found us, but he said that thing in the woods was probably following us and sent us to you, and ... I guess you know the rest."

"What happens now?" asked Alex.

Alex's words hung in the air, uncomfortable and unavoidable. *That's a really good question,* mused a thought in Joanne's head. She wanted to tell them everything would be alright. *But we're not going to know how fucked up this bundle is until Erica or Melissa can get here to check in on it. Even if I call them now, they're over an hour away. And in the meantime, whatever the hell they stole this thing from is probably pissed and on its way.* A little twitch across her tattoos gave her the impression it was closer than "on its way." Drafts of answers fluttered through her head as she tried to find the best way to frame the situation in an optimistic light. None of them felt right, but something had to be said (and done). Joanne picked one, cleared her throat, and leaned in over the table towards the trio while doing her best to not look at the macabre bundle of shadows still writhing on the table.

"Well, *now* you all do nothing but hole up tight down here," Joanne barked to fake a sense of confidence. Something about her own tone caught her off guard, instilled a sense of resolution in her chest. A fragment of a thought, the first stone in an avalanche of ideas, sprung into existence: the way her tattoos gurgled with palpable excitement gave her the impression the idea was not hers alone. "Do any of you all have phones that have a signal down here?"

The three of them checked, Dave, alone, giving an affirmative nod.

"Alright," she continued, snatching Dave's phone from across the table and finding the contacts. A sympathetic echo to the bundle's morbid energy assaulted her senses, sickly whispers of death pouring down the stairway and over Joanne's shoulders. "I'm going to give you a number. You call it; tell them Joanne told you to call and that there's an emergency at the vault. Got it?"

Dave again replied with a nod, taking back his phone with a quickness and looking at the new phone number. With a clip in her step, Joanne dashed into one of the half-cylinder alcoves along the wall, thankful for the first time that she had put so much effort into taking inventory. In a matter of seconds, the avalanche of ideas in her head had solidified into a plan. *A stupid plan, but if it works we knock out two birds with one stone.*

"That stick looking thing you took that item from is probably on its way, if it isn't already here," she yelled, avoiding absolutes in a vague hope it would bring comfort. "Don't ask how I know. Could be a monster, could be a demon, could be some ... other who-knows-what. There's a hell of a lot out there that just doesn't make sense. Whatever it is, I'm going to lock you in here and deal with it, or at least buy some time till the coven can get here, ok?"

Her eyes grazed over the menagerie of enchanted odds and ends on the overladen wooden shelves while she spoke, passing the jumbles of loose amulets, carved bones, and rune-etched slates before settling on a wooden staff just shy of her height. *A fitting choice,* whispered her inner monologue. Without hesitation, she plucked it from its resting place, wincing as the shallow runes along its surface clawed at her hands and threatened to draw blood. Biting her lip, Joanne pushed away the discomfort, taking a moment to marvel at her craftsmanship, allowing herself to ponder the weapon designed to end her life if she ever changed and didn't change back.

"While I'm gone, don't touch a fucking thing," Joanne concluded, turning to face the three at the table: confusion, incredulity, and panic drawn across their faces.

"Wait, that's crazy!" Alex yelled. "We saw the bodies. Morgan said it was huge! It's gonna go right through you, and we're gonna be stuck down here with no way out."

"I promise you, it's not getting down here. If I don't come back, someone will be by to let you out," Joanne shouted, shuddering as an uncomfortable jumble of nervousness and excitement bloomed in her core.

Beneath the surface of her skin, she felt a reservoir of untapped magic just waiting to be released. The thing bound in Joanne's tattoos tugged at her senses, its apparent eagerness to cooperate discomforting. Part of her wondered if it did so out of self-preservation, aware of what awaited her outside the vault or perhaps it had found a way to break its bonds. *This is a terrible fucking idea,* reiterated her inner monologue, *but if I'm gonna have to spend some of this magic at some point it may's well be now.*

Joanne took a deep breath and focused on her tattoos, bidding the entity bound within to share its power. Her muscles rippled beneath her skin in response, intoxicating strength filling her arms. Fear gripped her for a moment that the tattoos wouldn't hold, that she would succumb and change, that she would wake to the broken, half-devoured bodies of the three people she was trying to save. *No, I am in control,* she told herself, taking another deep breath, delving deeper into the well of magic. In a disorienting burst, the world around her became sharper and brighter as the shadows burned away. The sensory change reminded her of her first time drinking coffee, of that first overpowering feeling of alertness that no cup of coffee since had been able to replicate. She turned to Alex and the others, an exhilarating sense of energy and strength coursing through her, a tingling at her fingertips at the power beginning to spill from her tattoos.

"Make that phone call." She turned to the stairs, her staff clicking against the concrete with the heavy rhythm of determination.

"I'm going to rip whatever's up there to fucking shreds."

***

"*Ehedran!*"

Joanne watched the runes on the heavy, iron door burn with red flame for a brief moment before melting back into the smooth, cold gray surface. *Nothing's getting through that,* she thought with an air of smugness, tapping the metal with the butt of her staff for good measure. The clang of wood against metal bounced in her eardrums with unexpected ferocity. "Jeeze," she breathed through her clenched jaw, grinding her teeth as the ringing in her ears faded.

The expansion of sensations disoriented and exhilarated in equal degrees. Walking up the old stairs from the basement, the world around her felt alive with sights, sounds, and smells that before had been almost imperceptible: the delicate crunch of dust between her boots and the old wood; the damp, floral, stony scent of the ancient paint; the scamper of insects eking out their existence somewhere deep within the walls. Halfway up the stairs, fueled by her newfound senses, a conflagration of fear erupted in the pit of her stomach: what if she tapped too far into her newfound power? What would happen if she changed just enough to break the tattoos?

A flood of sounds and smells poured down the stairs above her, only adding to her fear: half-heard cracks of snapping branches settled in her ears, carried through the store on the back of the weeping wind; the dusty, thick, sweet smell of decaying meat and dying leaves flooded her nostrils, invoking disgust in her mind and a gurgling rumble of hunger in her stomach. A heavy sense of dreadful, morbid power bled into every corner of her consciousness, the same feeling radiating from the bundle but focused upon the blade of something's prying gaze. She knew it was waiting just outside. Instinct told Joanne it could sense her with as much clarity as she sensed it. There was no hiding, only delaying. The closer she got to the summit of the basement stairs the more she found her legs refusing her wishes to move forward. *You're gonna have to face it one way or another, you know,* chimed a pragmatic voice in her head, almost drowned in the thick drone of anxiety and panic. *It's waiting for you to make a move for now, but eventually it's going to try its luck against the wards on the windows.* The ominous tapping and scraping of wood against glass from above rattled in her ears, as if to fortify the point.

Joanne took a deep breath and then another. A chuckle escaped her lips thinking back to her firm words downstairs.

"I'm going to rip it to fucking shreds, hah," she mocked, "All bark and no bite, just putting on a show."

Eyeing her tattoos and the dancing light of magic along them, she flexed and stretched her limbs, bidding them to quit their cowardice and let her move forward. With as much instinct as breathing, she opened the imaginary valve of her magic, a cascade of worry followed by satisfaction as she felt her muscles shift and wriggle with greater intensity under her skin, soaking in the half-seen sparks of power. The feeling of growing strength was all she needed to ascend the last few stairs.

"Alright, Joanne, time to put your money where your mouth is."

It took her a moment to process what she saw past the windows, but once the image clicked, Joanne felt her heart drop with dread. Her intuition told her it was still dark, yet to her eyes, the world took on an uncanny sepia devoid of pure shadow. Outside, the light of the streetlamp glowed with the brightness of the sun in an overcast dawn, its light blanketing the heads of a mass of figures like a thin layer of snow. They stood motionless on the otherwise empty street, staring through the window. Reflected light sparkled against what remained of their eyes, but beyond that radiance there was no sparkle of life. As Joanne's gaze traveled across the throng, her dread mounted, her eyes picking at the signs of decay.

An overwhelming desire to flee tugged at her heels, but she pushed forward, the air feeling closer to rushing water against her shins as Joanne walked. Her skin crawled at the way the corpses' heads moved in unison to keep their lifeless eyes fixed on her. In the grim atmosphere, her footsteps thundered against the hardwood, the dead beyond without breath or heartbeat, the rest of the world seeming to curl away with anticipation. Joanne reached the door despite the dread, despite that whisper inviting the contemplation of death that even now persisted. It was hard to tell how many corpses stood before her: the first row stood at the curb, about a meter away from the storefront, but behind them the mass of bodies was hard to count.

A masochistic thought crept into her head as she stared at the decomposing bodies with their assortment of damages: *how many of them do you think you sent to the grave? How many are the bodies of the people you killed for sport alone?* She dismissed the thought, though not before she saw a skeletal cadaver whose ribs were carved with all too familiar gashes and tooth marks.

Movement from the top of the window sent Joanne jumping backwards, her heart leaping from the pit of her stomach with surprise. Another corpse, more fresh and intact than the others, descended into her field of view, all too much reminding her of the way she had made her action figures fly as a kid. She winced as it touched the ground, its bones making an audible *crack* as its legs made contact against the sidewalk with uncaring force. Goosebumps formed across her body as it looked at her, its eyes lifeless yet sparkling with an eldritch alertness.

Staring at her, it opened its mouth to speak, the muffled sound of popping joints and splitting flesh through the glass sending shivers through Joanne's body as the mouth was forced far too wide.

"You have ... something ... that is ... mine." The croaking voice washed through her core with a terrible chill. In the moment, it sounded human, but there was something alien in its undertone: as though something unfamiliar with the concept of speech was rummaging through the corpse's dead brain to find words that would best convey its desires. The ragdoll body cocked its head to the side, waiting for a response. For a flicker of a second, Joanne caught a sense of movement from behind and above. Shifting her focus from the corpse, a terrible realization struck her: she had been so focused on the corpse that she had not seen its puppeteer.

Morgan's description, though vague, was spot on. Above the corpses kneeled a crooked, headless figure shaped from innumerable branches tied together with sinew. In a vague, mocking way, it looked almost human: a headless, wicker person with a long, narrow torso and lanky arms and legs. Weathered, desiccated roots sprouted from where its hands and feet should have been. It reminded Joanne of a stick figure drawn by a child still new to art, ripped off the page and given life. Something about the way its wooden form played against the light made it hard to focus upon, made it hard to see where the body ended and the limbs began. It wasn't that it avoided illumination the way the bundle of morbidity did: rather, it seemed as if light itself died on contact with the cracked, chaotic spans of dry wood. She could hear it snap and groan with each movement as it hovered over the group of corpses, using its long arms to move its chosen puppet. Its creaking movements possessed a slow, unsettling purposefulness, reminding Joanne of the way a praying mantis sways to observe its prey. She shivered at the feeling of its gaze upon her, eyeless and sourceless beyond the beady eyes of its puppet. Everything about it felt cold, distant, ageless: the same feeling she got staring at the grave of someone long gone and long forgotten, reduced to a name and a date upon a soulless piece of granite.

The corpse in the entity's grasp shuffled forward a little. Joanne's skin crawled now that she saw the way the entity's roots wriggled inside the dead flesh to control its movement. With each passing moment, the being reminded her more of a giant child on their knees, toying with a doll worn to the point of breaking. For a moment, some morbid part of her mind wondered if submitting to its demands might grant her a more expeditious death, but something told her that mercy was a concept with which it was unfamiliar.

At a bare minimum, responding might buy me time to think this through, she thought, her hand moving to unlock the deadbolt of the door without any thought, *and at the very least, I should get out there so I don't have to order new windows in the morning. If I'm still in one piece.*

Joanne stepped outside, the gentle thud of the door closing behind her an uncomfortable reminder that going back would not be an option. Her skin prickled at the chill in the air, the intensity of the damp, moldy smell assaulting her nostrils. Joanne tried to roar with confidence but felt her voice crack with uncertainty.

"Oh, I have something of yours, do I? What exactly do you think I have?"

Making eye contact with the corpse turned her stomach, but somehow that felt more comfortable than trying to find any sort of face on the thing that towered over her.

There was no sign of recognition on the blank, broken face, yet after a moment, it gave her a reply.

"My focus. You cannot hide it. Give it to me."

Without a window between them, the crunching of bone and snapping of muscle and skin was unbearable–the wet, harsh sound crawling into her ears and squirming through her nervous system. *Some good news at least,* Joanne had to admit, a pinprick of relief gracing her spine with the knowledge that the bundle in the basement was little more than a battery. Before she could think any further, the forelimbs of the entity quivered and shifted before her, snapping and rattling with what sounded like impatience. *Guess talking isn't going to stall things after all. Am I really ready for this?*

"Suppose we're going to find out," she muttered to herself. Her muscles tensing, her grip tightening around the staff at her side, Joanne looked up to the faceless entity for one quick moment to steady herself before she yelled her defiances into the night. "I'll give you nothing, you fucking stick! The vault and its contents are mine to protect, so I kindly ask you to crawl back down whatever fucking roots you crawled up on. ***Veilchazad, Mnaic kthat!***"

With those last words, Joanne struck the staff against the concrete, grimacing at a flash of heat in her palm as the carved wooden pole splintered in her grip. For a second, there was nothing but the heavy echo of the words in her ears. A gripping panic seized her–panic that something had gone wrong and the invocation had failed. But the feeling subsided with a sudden change in the air, a growing feeling of static and the scent of smoldering copper. The sensations gave her just enough warning to cover her ears before the night sky emitted a low, furious growl. The corpse puppet looked into the air for its master. Joanne thought for a moment she could see surprise dawn upon the rotting face. But before the wicker creature could react, a spear of amber lightning crashed upon its long, narrow back, blinding in its ferocity as it pierced the being and froze into a sturdy beam of sparking fulgurite.

A violent shockwave hit Joanne, almost sending her flying. From somewhere above, she heard glass shatter, realizing only now that the conflict ahead was bound to draw attention. Dazed, Joanne saw the spindly branch limbs of the entity tugging to try and free itself from the new, stony anchor that held it in place, thick smoke billowing from the impact site. The spell possessed more power than she had anticipated, which was both satisfying and worrisome. Bringing out the big guns made things easier in the short term, but sooner or later *something* would catch the threads of **Power** on the wind and come around to see if it could be plundered.

A shrill whine flooded the air, bypassing Joanne's ears and burrowing straight into her skull. At the sound, the throng of corpses stood at attention, their bones crunching and snapping at the swiftness of their movement, their eyes sparking with fresh life in the dark. With uncanny synchronicity, the dead began to shamble towards her, joints creaking and grinding as they battled their independent levels of rigor mortis. In any other scenario, Joanne felt the sight of the walking dead would paralyze her. Now though, she found only excitement and a need to meet them head on. With a roar, she dropped what remained of the splintered staff and rushed into the hoard before her, her muscles burning and swelling beneath her skin, an unpleasant looseness building in her teeth and nails as new ones designed for rending and piercing threatened to push their way out.

Fear of losing control evaporated into bloodlust and fury. Joanne let herself go, her consciousness sitting in the back of her mind watching herself tear the corpses apart like sheets of paper, scattering the pieces across the asphalt. Her nose burned with the thick scent of rancid blood and bile and pulverized bone, the sounds of ripping cloth and flesh and the snap of flimsy rotting limbs beating upon her eardrums with a satisfying rhythm. It took all of her willpower to stop herself from crouching down to consume the bony chunks of rancid flesh as she fought. Watching herself wade through the helpless bodies towards the pinned entity, a sickening joy filled her: a primal ecstasy only found in the act of the hunt.

The dead tried to fight back, forcing their way towards her as if they were a singular blob-like creature: a wall of flesh, bone, torn clothes, and arms. Their frigid hands brushed against her skin with a chilling dampness, threatening to pin her down through sheer numbers. Yet their strength was for nought, and within moments Joanne had ripped a path through them, the uncomfortable feeling of new limbs, eyes, and mouths trying to burst from her back and sides as the entity bound within her sought greater control.

In a matter of seconds, she found herself standing at one of the massive legs of the entity, a steaming pile of shattered corpses in her wake, the splintering branches of its form slick with the blood of its followers. Not stopping to consider the size difference, Joanne seized it with her slippery hands, seeking places where she could find a firm grip. Bitter cold burned her fingers as they slipped in between the broken branches and their sinew bindings, but she persisted, digging deeper and forcing all her power forward. Despite her rage, she found herself wishing to recoil as her fingers cut against things that felt like teeth deep within the being's limb. Yet despite that desire she did not relent, pushing her way into its crevices until she found a sturdy handhold.

She pulled. A horrible scream filled her ears as she ripped a chunk from the creature, a cry of pain which sounded almost human but had no source. The entity recoiled, lashing out with its remaining stub of a leg and sending Joanne flying a few meters. The instincts of her possessor jumped into play: with lightning speed beyond her mental acuity, she found herself curling and twisting in the air, surprise and satisfaction giving her a warm feeling as she tucked and rolled into an easy landing. A flickering light caught her eye, her heart thundering in her chest as adrenaline began to catch up with her. Across the sea of broken bodies, the entity writhed against its fulgurite restraint, unhealthy orange flames dancing at her spell's point of impact upon its spindly torso. Amidst its flailing, it had torn its puppet in half, the empty, broken torso dancing in the air, the dislocated jaw bouncing at wild angles until being freed from the rest of the face with a wet, shearing sound. For a moment, the head lolled to the side to face Joanne, the look of raw anger in its eyes sending a sickening shiver across her neck.

In the distance behind her, Joanne picked up the holler of sirens, their volume ebbing before growing once more as her senses dulled and returned to normal. Stretching to stand up straight she felt her strength wane, replaced by splitting pain and exhaustion as the last of her stored **Power** trickled into the earth. Watching the thing before her squirming as flames consumed more of its body, a weary smile found its way onto her face. *You didn't change,* she thought in amazement. A wave of relief and joy filled her heart, overflowing through her body till tears of joy welled in her eyes. The choking, gritty feel of smoke hit the back of her throat, carried away from the mass of branches as they collapsed and shuddered with ever more feeble twitches. A flashing blue and red light grew around her upon the road, competing with the illumination of the streetlamps, amplifying the crimson sheen of blood and gore. Joanne cringed at the sound of tires crunching against bone and the whine of breaks, followed by the click of a car door.

"Well, uh ... honestly not what I was expecting," said a familiar baritone voice a meter from her ear. Joanne did not turn to acknowledge Lucas's presence, her eyes fixed on the burning wicker figure as its last twitches ceased. "Station got a call that there was a 'riot:' glass breakin', sound of fighting, fires," he continued, his short, broad profile coming into view in Joanne's peripheral. "I pulled some strings, worked some magic. Charms should wear off in a few hours. Should give us plenty of time to clean up before ..."

"Us?" interjected Joanne, turning to Lucas, some lingering aspect of primal wrath still flowing in her nerves as she stared daggers. "No. *You're* cleaning up," she shouted, grabbing the store key from her pocket and thrusting it into his hand. "And then when *you're* done, *you're* going down into the vault to take care of those kids and that focus you sent along with them. Got it?"

Lucas responded with a feeble, resigned nod.

"As for me ..." she continued, shouting in no direction in particular, walking with care through the ruined bodies, trying her best not to slip on festering entrails or chunks of bone. "I'm going back to fucking bed."

Without another word, Joanne wrenched open the door that led to her studio apartment and slammed it shut behind her, leaving Lucas a road littered with broken corpses and the fresh light of dawn.

HIS CASTLE CRUMBLES

He wanders the halls of his castle.

Unease stalks him, leers at him from every corner as he walks laps through the squared-off corridors. A cocktail of worry, doubt, and dreadful anticipation boils in his mind, his eyes unable to avoid glancing at the ornate, ivory stucco and gilded pillars around him.

There are cracks in the walls: faint fractures, minor blemishes upon the otherwise pristine stucco. Despite their negligible severity, each one drives another nail of despair into his turbulent thoughts.

"Where are you?" he asks the rows of gilded pillars. "Why are you silent?"

He expects an answer. His ears stand alert, seeking those familiar, tiny whispers scratching at the masonry behind the stucco. His jaw clenches in hopeful anticipation for those heavy hands that so often come to rest on his shoulders, visible only in the corners of his eyes.

Instead, there is only a brooding, unfamiliar quiet, punctuated by the soft tap of his leather soles upon the dense burgundy carpet. His senses stand on edge, amplified by a lack of something on the edge of tangibility: the darkness that exists within a well-lit room, only revealed when the light is extinguished; the sounds and smells just beyond the boundaries of perception. Neither are quite akin to what he feels, but they're the closest he can get to describing the presence of his Patron.

He walks onward, restarting the loop around his castle once more. The dark, webbed cracks eye him as if contemplating malice: he swears they are in different places each time he makes a full circle of the hallway. Shadows coalesce above him, peering from the vaulted ceiling and its soaring arches, their edges glinting with a knife's sharpness. Static lurks in every crease of his luxurious, sea-blue robe, lashing out against his arms with every shuffling step he takes. The faint, woody, sweet smell of sandalwood incense wafts past his nostrils, sourceless and omnipresent, tinged with an earthy hint of rot.

It's not the first time it has been distant for a while, he tries to rationalize. The thought elicits a flinch at the corners of his lips, his mind dredging up memories of those weeks of profound silence: memories of the way the castle began to collapse whenever his Patron was distant. Often, it would return as swift as it had left, the damage vanishing as though it had never occurred. *But sometimes ...*

His eyes twitch, an instinctual response to the remembered rage and accusations dangled over his head, empty of reason, pushed upon his shoulders without an explanation of how to restore his Patron's graces. How long had he spent in those moments before its shrine, tears searing his cheeks as he tried every plea and offering he could in hope of appeasing it.

Perhaps I've done something wrong. Perhaps the sacrifices are not enough?

Spurred onward by his worry, his thoughts wander back to his last offering. He turns over the details of the ritual in his mind, puzzling over the fuzzy images drawn from vaults in his memory he would prefer to not have to open.

I placed the incense as it instructed, he ruminates, going through his checklist, unaware of how many times he has repeated this exercise today. *The brass bowl, the inscribed circlets, I remember placing them. The incantation ...*"

**"Echlas, mnaig. Echlas, drothoag. Echlas, ehedran scraithe gnazh ...*"

The eager words spill from his tongue, pooling at his feet. Goosebumps ripple across his skin as his voice freezes the air around him, subtle **Power** casting its silent echo throughout his castle.

"I did say it right, didn't I?"

Again, he waits: waits for the whispers in his footsteps, waits for half-seen lips in his peripheral to hum their affirmations into his ear. Again, only silence answers, mocking quiet spat from the grinning fractures in the walls as they shed their jagged, chipping stucco teeth upon the burgundy carpet.

For a moment, he contemplates visiting the altar room to take action, to broadcast his plea for contact from his Patron.

"Not yet, give it time." he whispers to himself. His mind wades deeper into the mire of rumination. Each footfall against the thick weave of the burgundy carpet dredges up images of his last offering for him to sift through: the way fear and confusion danced across her face as the sedatives wore off. The way her scream echoed through the altar room as her hands took a mind of their own, tearing the flesh from her body piece by piece, casting it into the offering bowl until there was nothing left for her to give.

He shudders, a lance of guilt stabbing his side for the first time he could remember in recent history. *I should have kept looking for a different one: she was too much like the first*. Hollow discomfort blooms in his mind as he tries to remember more about the first. *What was her name, again?*

The balcony that oversees the courtyard comes into view as he rounds the corner, pulling him from his thoughts. A desire for a change of pace draws him to break his endless loop and step out into the night.

He leans against the railing, trying his best to ignore the chips and discoloration on the delicate, marble latticework. The vast courtyard stretches out before him, its walls a tangle of sharp spires and twisting buttresses: flocks of grotesques occupy the ledges, their blurry, shapeless granite forms watching over the midnight gardens; rays of amber light shine from many rows of narrow windows; the peel of distant wind chimes sing, defying the absence of the wind, their whimsical melodies dancing in the night sky.

He considers the gardens, continents of green skirted by weaving marble paths and elegant sapphire fountains. Relief fills him to see them in their usual pristine condition. His eyes rest on the soothing contours of the manicured trees, their fat twisted trunks slithering into canopies of dark green, unmoving leaves. The flowers catch his gaze. On a whim, he commands them to put on a display, fireworks of violet and amethyst sparkling in series among the well-manicured grass and trained hedges, fluttering into the air with the grace of lunar moths. His vision climbs to follow the colorful lights, savoring the reprieve from his anxiety that comes from watching them dance into the night sky. The void above draws his attention. Within its endless darkness hang countless planets, motionless, silent, their geography illuminated by lightless, dead stars.

Unbridled awe warms his body as he stares into space, a weightless sense of wonder undiluted by the many times he has witnessed this view. For the first time this night, his mind unwinds, anxiety loosening its vicious grip. *How far you have come from being an underpaid, overworked accountant from Queens.* That hell of grating, syncopated phones and furious tapping of keyboards manifests in his mind's eye: that nightmare of morgue-white, soulless cubicles and desiccated air tainted with carpet cleaning fluid; that dead jungle he dragged himself to endure every week, returning home with only enough to keep some food in his belly and a roof over his head.

A smile crosses his lips, his Patron's first whisper echoing in his memory. *I'm here,* it had said in a clear, kind voice, almost imperceptible against the hum of the city night as he lay in bed, staring at the ceiling. He remembers that spark of surprised joy, the immediate flush of ecstasy from a lover's touch. He had so often cried out to be heard, to receive the affirmation that *something* bigger than he was there, was listening: but never had he expected it to answer.

His eyes trace the dead worlds above him as his thoughts wander among the memories of his Patron's gifts and boons: the castle in which he now stands; the vast bookshelves of tomes and objects of **Power** that lie in his study, an arsenal of knowledge and magic at his beck and call. *Whether it comes back with anger or not, it always returns with bountiful gifts,* he reminds himself. A new excitement bubbles up within his mind, excitement for what wonders his Patron will bring him.

"I promise when you're back to offer a grand sacrifice," he says into the calm air, hoping vocalizing his thoughts might call its attention and bring it back sooner. Having his fill for the splendor of the gardens he turns back to his castle, his step lighter, his shoulders less burdened.

But the feeling of relief is short.

Something is different when he steps foot within the halls.

The air is heavier. It weighs upon his shoulders, tightens around his throat. His eyes dart around the corridor. The cracks in the walls have expanded, growing from spider-web-fine fractures to thick, dark gouges in the stucco that reveal bone-white stones and bloody mortar. His nostrils wince at a cold, ill breeze wafting past his face, carrying with it unpleasant, all too familiar smells: stale tobacco, dusty black mold clinging to the feet of plastic shower curtains, muted floral tones of cheap laundry detergent on moth chewed clothing. Sounds creep into his ears, the faint scraping and tapping of fingernails clawing at gritty cement from behind the ivory stucco and gilded pillars.

"Is that you?" he asks.

A wordless, silent roar of unquenchable rage boils down the hall, a scream of liquid hatred that crushes against his body. And then utter emptiness. An emptiness that defies the boundaries of the material world around him, that renders the air hollow, that sucks the soul from the spectrum of color. He shivers, sweat freezing on his brow, the distillate of his fear and anxiety rushing through him as realization dawns upon him.

His Patron has abandoned him.

His castle crumbles.

"No! Wait! Come back and tell me what I must do, I beg you," he yells, the sound of his voice dying on the stale air. He runs, offers rushing through his mind, a laundry list of pleas: *more sacrifice, more prayer, more adoration. Anything it wants.* The crunch of stucco under his feet jars his bones with every step, the burgundy carpet spotted with a heavy snow of ivory flakes.

Within a moment, the grand hall is before him, the imposing, hewn oak double doors to the altar room at the far end. His eyes catch the once opulent chandeliers as he rushes forward, their usual inner light extinguished. The cold on his brow turns to nausea, a sickening, clammy pall draped over his body that presses heavier upon him with each step, his mind once more cast into churning over every mistake.

He reaches the heavy doors, pulling them open, coughing at the rust and termite dust that invades his nostrils. An involuntary gasp of surprise flies from his tongue as the altar room comes into view. When before the Patron had held its anger over him, when the castle around him had begun to wither, the altar room alone had remained flawless. But now, ruins stand before him: the once graceful rib cage of arches holding up the ceiling glares at him from the shadows with countless, deep pockmarks, their faces aged with thick beards of sickly moss; massive tapestries, woven pieces of art commissioned at the whim of his patron, hang ragged, picked apart by moths, dotted with dark, pustulent scabs; the intricate mosaic floor hosts corpulent, misshapen hands of fungi, growing and dying before his eyes, tracing their fingers through a mist of spores.

And in the center stands the altar, his Patron's shapeless likeness carved in amber: flawless still, but now lifeless. The final, white hot nail driving home his abandonment.

The ground trembles. Panic biting at his heels, he flees the altar, mold and soft chunks of pitted marble raining down upon his shoulders, the hewn oak doors closing behind him with a solemn *thud*. He looks back on instinct, his chest heaving, his eyes darting across the wall where the door should be. Sickening recognition strikes him as his eyes catch the small details of that wall: the familiar tear in the drab wallpaper, the scratches and dents in the drywall, the stains from spilled liquor and tobacco smoke.

His castle crumbles.

He runs from the grand hall, navigating the darkening halls to the study. A faint hope lingers that perhaps something may be salvaged in the wreckage. But the garden has claimed the study as its own, the shelves consumed by broad, smooth, twisted trunks pulsing with some mockery of a heartbeat. His hands float to grasp his hair, his mind seized by a dull burning sensation of loss, his ears flood with the tear of paper and the crunch of metal as the trees constrict his collection of tomes and artifacts. "No, no no no no," he pants, his breath in time with his footsteps, the slap of his soles against failing marble interjected with soft crunches and squeals of fat grass and mushrooms under his heels.

"What did I do wrong? I followed every instruction! Why are you doing this?"

His castle crumbles.

The study collapses into a tangle of groaning roots. He abandons it to its fate, stumbling once more through those old, familiar hallways. Where the hallway should turn before him, there is now only an endless corridor of crumbling stucco and tarnished pillars. Arms push through the cracks in the stucco in the dozens, their long fingers digging into the walls, ripping away the plaster, wrestling the stone blocks from their mortar before retreating back into the walls. Paralyzed, he stares as piece by piece they disassemble his castle. An end to the hall comes into view, an all too familiar surface of torn wallpaper and dented drywall approaching at a breakneck pace.

"Please, no, please! Just tell me what you want!" he sobs, tears burning against his cheeks, the last of the carpet pulled out from under his feet, the last of the gold pillars melting before his eyes.

"Tell me what you want! Tell me what you want!"

It is not silence that answers him but the angry rattle of a train passing; the screams of ambulances, banshees in the night; the stench of cigarette smoke fused into old paint and floorboards rotted by alcohol; the flicker of the singular lightbulb above him, signaling its inevitable failure.

He stares at the old, empty, one room apartment: the pathetic space where his castle once stood. His eyes catch the chalk circle surrounding him on the irregular wood floor. His gaze travels across the intricate rows of characters within its circumference, settling upon the dusty, rotten remains of his first offering. *Elizabeth. Her name was Elizabeth.* He grasps at the roots that strangle the dusty corpse, one last echo of the **Power** that had once run through them vibrating across his skin before they slink back into the floorboards. In his hands, the corpse disintegrates, the simple gold band he had once slipped on her finger the only thing to remain.

Hot lines draw themselves upon his cheeks; a tickle in his throat precurses a scream of grief. The departure of his shock takes his strength.

He crumbles, his body collapsing into pitiful sobs that fall upon all too many unlistening, uncaring ears.

No, something does listen, an instinct tells him. In the furthest corners of his hearing, something whispers: a voice slithering just within the cries of a nearby infant and the shouts of couples within inches of violence. A glint of recognition tugs at his spine.

"Are you there?" he asks, the words stinging his throat between sobs.

I'm here.

"Please. Tell me what you want."

No words prick at his ears in reply: only the soft flap of something wet falling upon solid ground. The damp sound bores into his skull, its meaning all too clear. He blinks, and before him is the brass bowl and engraved circlets. A fog of incense smoke caresses his knees.

Flesh. Flesh for his castle.

His hand shakes, climbing upward to press against his jaw. How many times has he witnessed what he now performs upon himself? His mind recoils with anticipation for the pain, his fingers finding purchase around his cheek, nails pinching at the skin. He feels the warmth of his Patron fill his hands, imbue them with strength. With a scream he pulls, his efforts rewarded by the wet snap of muscle and burning nerves and the shock of frigid air against his exposed tongue. In shock, he considers the squirming chunk of his own skin and flesh gripped in his hand before raising it aloft, an offering to his Patron. Delighted relief returns. His gift of flesh flutters from his grasp, transfigured into a scrap of familiar, burgundy carpet.

More.

With a viscous stab of pain and a sucking pop, he tears his eyes from his sockets and tosses them onto the floor. In a moment of vertigo, his disembodied vision spins and turns to face his body, the voice demanding that he watch as he tears off handfuls of flesh. Despite the pain, a laugh of joy escapes the holes in his cheeks as each offering replaces a fragment of carpet, a ruddy brick, a glinting sheet of fresh stucco.

More.

Pain and ecstasy melt together, his body piece by piece losing feeling as his fingers rip the skin and meat from his bones. A burning cold racks his chest, morbid fascination numbing his mind, realizing that it is the first time his lungs have felt fresh air on the outside. Piece by piece by piece, he rebuilds his castle, till his fingers rake against bone, till his abdominal muscles are torn away and he feels himself relieved of the weight of his organs, his eyes entombed by an avalanche of his innards.

All, he is told, and all he gives, till he is nothing but a pain maddened brain entombed within a ragged, crimson pile of bones. His skeletal hands slip against the slick surface of his ribcage, compelled to complete their task by a will beyond his own as they pick at the last scraps of flesh.

His final howls echo through the lonely halls of his castle, painting the stucco walls and gilded pillars with his agony.

ABOUT THE AUTHOR

 Bert S. Lechner is an author on the autism spectrum born and raised near San Francisco, California. He studied music at the University of Puget Sound in Tacoma, Washington, originally dreaming of becoming a composer before discovering a passion for writing and telling stories. After years of pursuing different lines of work, from wine salesperson to IT specialist, Bert finally decided to pursue his passion for writing and to begin publishing his works.

When he's not writing, Bert can be found cooking, making cheese, spending time with his cats, reading, or playing video games, quite often simultaneously.

Made in the USA
Columbia, SC
21 October 2024

44812672R00087